THABANG H.A MATHAPO

MOYA

Letters of African urban legends

VOL: 1

First Edition©

Thabang H.A Mathapo.

ISBN: 978-0-620-92879-3

DISCLAIMER ©.

This book is dedicated to:

This book is dedicated to my family and most importantly my mother who has raised me to become a man of good character and of respectable integrity.

My mother taught me the true meaning of sacrifice, diligence, and responsibility.

With these tools, I matured well and became spiritually evolved from a young age.

Thank You, mother

I love you.

TABLE OF CONTENTS

Introduction

Dear Son,

I can feel that you are getting stronger day by day. I am extremely proud of not only you but of the rest of your brothers and sisters across the continent and the globe. There is much you do not understand, and much to learn. You will be experiencing unusual changes for the next 12 years of your life. We are now in the Age of Aquarius which means the creator will be handing down new knowledge to the ancestors so that they can refresh your Moya with enlightenment.

This may cause illness and confusion within you...

Visions will make themselves known to you as you delve deeper within the esoteric realms of spirituality. I urge you to stay calm and remember to express these epiphanies through writing in your journal. I expect you to write letters to me and mail them via the post office.

I know you are young and don't understand why...

There is an energy present within the skill of penmanship and the spiritual connection between a student and master strengthens when they write each other letters by hand. I will also be using the post office to send you newspaper articles from an independent provincial publication that was established by students from all over South Africa during the 1976 uprising. Today it is run by University students who have international partners from all over the globe who report on paranormal events.

Note: Please pardon the grammar and vocab as this publication is not written by professionals.

I could only send you pieces of stories so you will have to conduct further research.

They are young...

I urge you to be patient as I am traveling between realms in pursuit of spiritual tools of war so that we can prepare for the war against the brothers and sisters of darkness. Remember that they have power only in the minds of their subjects. I have sent you a candle to help you balance the dark forces with the light.

I will pray for you so that you can be visited by mystics and griots of Moya who have come before you. Some will speak through your body and some will communicate via your Moya.

You are about to gain wisdom...

Try not to be consumed by power and give in to the

shadow. They will try their best to tempt you. Stay true to the creator as they live inside your soul.

Do not trust anyone.

P.S It is advisable that you also detail your dreams in a dream diary/journal.

The creator speaks to Southern Africans by way of dreams.

Regards, Mkhulu

''The all is mind. The universe is mental' -
African principle of Tehuti

Dream Diary Entry

Dream Title:

What was the dream about?

Where it took place:

My interpretation:

Keywords/phrases spoken within the dream:

Dream symbols:

Note to Self:

Azanian Ti

By Mbali Maboa, February 4, 2008

Two Vagina's and five chil

This is how I grew up, says Lerato Ngema, a 28 year old woman who was born with a female birth defect called uterus didelphys. This causes a biological mutation whereby the reproductive system is split into two sets. Lerato has conceived five children between the ages of 14 months and 6 years. The international health community has stated that this phenomena is not common. Less than 4000 women are actually living with this condition. The aspiring musician was diagnosed when she was 15 years old when she was rushed to hospital after a serious abdominal pain which resulted in bleeding. Without surgery at a young age she would not be able to have children in the future but the risks of her being internally damaged during intercourse could give her health complications. But as a devoted Christian she believed that god would bless her with offspring. But right after studying music in Cape Town she decided to take her relationship with her boyfriend to the next level.

Azanian Ti

By Maria Adams, February 13, 2008

Ph.D. Scientist sentenced h

Professor Xi Ming from the Chinese laboratory of human evolution has refused all allegations against him but has been charged for embezzling millions of dollars on a cloning machine. Between June 2006 and August 2007, Professor Ming (internationally respected for his scientific research in animal cloning and genetic manipulation) took (in his words) 43 million Yuan in government grant money and said he "invested" it in offshore corporations in the western hemisphere that he and his assistant (Cho Tran) had created to expound on their facilities where human blood was harvested. Ming further testified that he was going to conduct research which required human blood to make scientific strides in his research. He also explained how he was planning on experimenting on DNA found on a certain meteorite given to him by an unknown American billionaire. Ming is said to be convicted for 20 years on money laundering and other illegal scientific charges. Su Cheng, Ming's lawyer, tells Azanian Times that Li may appeal.

CHAPTER 1

SHOES' ARE HUNG ON STREET CABLES

DEAR MKHULU,

I FOLLOWED YOUR INSTRUCTIONS AND COMPLETED THE TASK THAT WAS REQUIRED OF ME TO CONDUCT THIS WEEKEND. THE LADY I WAS SENT TO HEAL RESIDES AT A SMALL INFORMAL TOWNSHIP CALLED NDLOVUVILLE RIGHT IN THE OUTSKIRTS OF RURAL KWA ZULU NATAL. SHE WAITED FOR ME AT NDLOVUVILLE PLAZA OUTSIDE THE CHISANYAMA ON THE CORNER OF GAZI AVENUE AND LUNGILE STREET. SHE SAT ON THE BENCH ANXIOUSLY AS I APPROACHED HER WHILE CROSSING THE STREET FROM THE PARKING LOT. AS I STRODE TOWARDS THE EATERY AND INTO THE SITTING AREA, A STRONG AROMA OF BRAAI MEAT AND A WEIRD STENCH OF SOAP WATER FROM THE CAR WASH FOAM HIT ME.

SINCE IT WAS CHILLY THAT MORNING I SUGGESTED THAT WE BE GIVEN A TABLE INSIDE THE RESTAURANT ON THE CORNER SOFA, SO WE COULD SPEAK IN PRIVATE.

WE EXCHANGED GREETINGS AND SHE ORDERED TWO COFFEE FOR US AS SHE BEGAN TO EXPLAIN WHY SHE SENT ME THE WHATSAPP MESSAGE.

MKHULU, WHAT I HEARD NEXT WOULD EVEN SURPRISE YOU.

THE LADY PAINFULLY STAMMERED HER WORDS IN NERVOUSNESS AS SHE EXPLAINED TO ME WHAT HAD HAPPENED TO HER SON SFISO. SFISO WAS A STREET DANCER WHO WAS PART OF A VERY POPULAR DANCE CREW CALLED "THE AMA 18". THE CREW DREW ITS NAME FROM A COMMON INTEREST OF AGE AND THEM BEING MATRIC LEARNERS MEETING EACH OTHER IN THE SAME YEAR FROM DIFFERENT SCHOOLS.

THEY WERE 3 STYLISH MATRIC STUDENTS IN SIMILAR HEIGHT, COMPLEXION, AND LANKY TALLNESS WHICH COULD BE EASILY DISTINGUISHED AS THEY WORE SKINNY FITTED CLOTHING. OUT OF THIS GROUP OF THREE, SFISO STOOD OUT AND HAD THE X-FACTOR BECAUSE HE WAS THE MAIN CHOREOGRAPHER OF THE LOT.

MUCH OF THE DANCE MOVES CAME FROM SFISO'S INNATE SKILL OF MIXING MULTIPLE TYPES OF DANCE GENRES. HE WOULD MIX VHOSHO WITH THE MOONWALK AT THE END AND HAVE CROWDS EXPLODING IN WHISTLES.

A DEEP PASSION THAT LAID WITHIN HIM TO RAISE MONEY TO BEGIN HIS STUDIES AT WITS UNIVERSITY IS WHAT MOTIVATED SFISO TO PERFORM ON THE LEVEL THAT HE DID.

THE LADY CONTINUED TO SAY THAT SFISO ALWAYS BELIEVED THAT HIS TALENT CAME FROM HIS SHOES', WHICH WERE GIVEN TO HIM BY HIS GRANDMOTHER AS A BIRTHDAY GIFT AT HIS SIXTH BIRTHDAY

PARTY BACK WHEN HE WAS A TWEEN.

THESE SHOES SHE MADE FOR HIM WERE BOUGHT FROM LEATHER SOLD AT THE NDLOVU MUTI MARKET AS HE COULD NOT AFFORD TO PURCHASE A NEW PAIR OF SHOES FOR DANCING. SHE LOVED HIM DEARLY AND WANTED HER GRANDSON TO ACCOMPLISH HIS DREAM OF MAYBE ONE DAY OPENING A DANCE ACADEMY IN ALL THE TOWNSHIPS OF MZANSI.

GOGO BELIEVED THAT THE SHOES WOULD GROW WITH HIM EVERY NIGHT AS HE SLEPT AND WOULD SPEAK TO HIM AT NIGHT TO GUIDE HIS CAREER BY WALKING THE PATH CHOSEN FOR HIM BY HIS ANCESTORS. SFISO CONSTANTLY TOLD HIS MOTHER THAT HE WOULD SOMETIMES WAKE UP IN THE MIDDLE OF THE NIGHT AND FEEL A DEEP HEATED BURN UNDER HIS FEET AS IF HE JUST WALKED ON THE SCORCHING SUMMER PAVEMENT OF NDLOVUVILLE DURING DECEMBER.

SHE THEN DISCLOSED THAT SHE DID NOT TAKE HIM SERIOUSLY AT FIRST. THIS WAS VERY INTERESTING TO HEAR BECAUSE I HAVE ONCE HEARD A SIMILAR EVENT HAPPENING TO SOMEONE ELSE BACK AT HOME...

BUT ANYWAY, LET'S CONTINUE WITH THE STORY...

SHE KEPT SHAKING AS SHE SPOKE ABOUT THE SHOES AND WOULD

DEEPLY LOOK INTO MY EYES THINKING I HAVE THE ANSWERS TO HER DILEMMA. SHE THEN SPOKE ABOUT AN EVENT THAT HAPPENED A WHILE BACK IN WHICH SFISO AND HIS DANCING FRIENDS ORGANIZED A MATRIC FAREWELL PARTY, INVITING ALL THE DANCE ENTHUSIASTS OF NDLOVUVILLE AT THE END OF THE NOVEMBER MATRIC EXAM SEASON JUST BEFORE THE DECEMBER HOLIDAYS BEGAN.

SHE APPROVED THE IDEA AND GAVE HIM SOME MONEY FOR POSTERS AND TO PAY FOR THE DJ.

THE EVENT WAS THEN SCHEDULED TO HAPPEN AT THE LOCAL PARK/SPORTS FIELD, ON A SATURDAY AFTERNOON. SFISOS' MOM COULDN'T ATTEND THE EVENT AS SHE WAS WORKING A DOUBLE SHIFT AT A RETAIL CLOTHING STORE A FEW BLOCKS FROM THE PLAZA. BUT THE BOYS BEING MINORS, NEEDED SOMEONE OLDER TO PRESIDE OVER THEIR EVENT. SHE ASKED HER NEIGHBOUR'S NIECE (GLORIA) TO MONITOR THE BOYS AT THE EVENT.

WHILE AT WORK, GLORIA CALLED HER WITH DISTURBING NEWS ABOUT WHAT HAD TAKEN PLACE AT THE EVENT. BEFORE SHE CONTINUED THE STORY, I TOLD HER TO EXPLAIN WHAT SHE EXPERIENCED IN THE EARLY HOURS OF THE MORNING ON THE DAY OF THE DANCE EVENT.

MOYA WANTED TO KNOW ABOUT HER STORY FROM HER PERSPECTIVE BEFORE SOMEONE ELSE'S TO AVOID BLAME AND CONFUSION.

APPARENTLY, SHE HEARD VOICES COMING FROM SFISOS' BEDROOM THAT MORNING.

SHE WOKE UP AND OPENED THE DOOR AND SAW SFISO ON THE FLOOR WITH SWEAT ALL OVER HIS BODY AND BLOOD UNDER HIS FEET.

TERRIFIED BY THIS, SHE QUICKLY GRABBED A THICK BLANKET AND COVERED HIM, REACHED FOR HER PHONE AND CALLED AN AMBULANCE. SFISO GOT UP AND JOKINGLY SHRUGGED IT OFF, CONVINCING HIS MOTHER THAT HE WAS DOING PUSH UP'S TO PHYSICALLY PREPARE HIM FOR THE DAY. THEY BOTH LAUGHED IT OFF AND PREPARED FOR THEIR DAY.

AS SHE EXPLAINED HER SIDE OF THIS MYSTERIOUS STORY, MOYA WHISPERS IN MY EAR AND REVEALED THAT GLORIA TOLD HER THAT WHEN THE EVENT STARTED SHE SAW SFISO AT THE BACK OF THE TOILET AREA (AT THE SPORTS FIELD) SPEAKING WITH FOUR OLDER MEN WHO SEEMED TO BE AGGRESSIVE TOWARDS HIM.

MINUTES LATER THE LADY TELLS ME THAT HER SON SHOWED NO SIGNS OF FEAR THE MORNING HE LEFT FOR THE EVENT. AROUND 10:15 P.M. SHE RECEIVED A PHONE CALL FROM SFISOS: DANCE FRIEND "KHALIPA" WHO TOLD HER THAT SFISO HAS GONE MISSING AND THAT A MYSTERIOUS BLACK CITI GOLF WAS LAST SEEN WITH HIM INSIDE.

SHE QUICKLY REACTED AND LEFT THE BUS STOP QUEUE AND GOT ON THE NEXT TAXI SHE COULD FIND AND RUSHED TO THE EVENT SITE TO SEE WHAT HAD GONE ON. THE TAXI MOVES CLOSER TOWARDS THE SPORTS FIELD AND SLOWLY DRIVES THROUGH A COLLAGE OF YOUNG PEOPLE SCATTERED ACROSS THE ENVIRONMENT, SOME OF WHICH ARE STANDING ON THE WALLS OF HOUSES AROUND THE FIELD.

PEOPLE:S FACES – LIKE THEY HAVE SEEN A GHOST ARE FRIGHTENED FROM GAZING AT THE POLICE VEHICLES WHILE WEARING NIGHTGOWNS AND STOCKINGS ON THEIR HEADS. SHE GETS OFF AT THE ENTRANCE AND RUNS TIRELESSLY AT THE POLICE AND THERE SHE FINDS SFISOS: FRIENDS, GLORIA, AND THE POLICE OFFICER WITH HANDS ON THEIR CHEEKS (JAWS WIDE OPEN IN DISBELIEF) AND ARMS ABOVE THEIR HEADS.

THE POLICE OFFICER SWITCHES ON THE SIREN AND EXPLAINS TO HER THAT SFISO IS MISSING BUT HIS SHOES HAVE BEEN FOUND INSIDE A BLACK CITI GOLF ALONGSIDE FOUR DEAD CRIMINALS WHOSE FEET HAVE BEEN CHOPPED OFF.

TRUTH OR MYTH

In Nile Valley civilizations like Nubia, shoes were considered sacred pieces of art as they connected the human body to the earth. The heel is today called the sole.

ASTONISHED AS THEY WERE, THEY HEADED FOR THE POLICE STATION. A MISSING PERSON'S CASE WAS OPENED AND A CRIMINAL INVESTIGATION WAS UNDERWAY.

AFTER A MONTH OF SEARCHING WITH NO LUCK, SHE DECIDES TO DECLARE HER SON DECEASED. TO MOURN HER SON, SHE KEPT HIS SHOES BESIDE THE BED IN HIS BEDROOM. A COUPLE OF MONTHS PASS AND SHE RECEIVES A MESSAGE FROM SFISO IN A DREAM SAYING HE IS NOT DEAD AND HE IS NOT ALIVE, HE WAS ATTACKED AND STABBED BY THOSE MEN FOR HIS SHOES.

THEY COULD NOT TAKE THE SHOES BECAUSE HIS GRANDMOTHER'S SPIRIT PROTECTED THEM THROUGHOUT THE CONFLICT SO THEY CHOPPED OFF HIS FEET WITH AN AXE WHILE HE WAS STILL ALIVE.

HE FURTHER TOLD HIS MOTHER THAT HE PASSED OUT AND WOKE UP AFTER BEING STRUCK. TO HIS SURPRISE, THE FOUR MEN DIED AND HE COULD SEE HIS BODY LAY BESIDE THEM AT THE OPEN FIELD WHERE THIS MURDER ATTEMPT HAPPENED 20KM AWAY.

SFISO TOLD HER THAT HE IS UNABLE TO CROSSOVER AND HIS BODY WILL REMAIN MISSING BECAUSE HE WAS MURDERED WITH THE SHOES ON HIS FEET BUT CUT FROM HIS BODY. SHE SAID THAT HIS SPIRIT IS IN HIS SHOES AND THAT HE CAN ONLY CROSSOVER WHEN THE SOLES OF THE SHOES ARE HEATED AT THE EARLY HOURS OF THE DAY.

THIS COULD BE BECAUSE SFISOS: RITUAL WAS TO WAKE UP EARLY IN THE MORNING TO PRACTICE FOR THE DAY. THIS WOULD THEN CAUSE A SPIRITUAL MANIFESTATION OF HIS GRANDMA:S SPIRIT TO EMERGE RESULTING IN HOT FLUSHES IN HIS LEGS.

SFISO THEN FURTHER EXPLAINED THAT FOR THIS TO HAPPEN SHE SHOULD WAKE UP EVERY MORNING AND TOSS THE PAIR OVER A STREET CABLE, WITH THE LACES TIED INTO A KNOT. THIS WILL ALLOW THE SUN TO HEAT THE SHOES SO THAT HE CAN USE ITS ENERGY TO RUN TOWARDS THE SPIRITUAL GATEWAY AND MAKE HIS TRANSITION BEFORE THE OLD LADY:S SPIRIT KEEPS HIS SOUL IN HIS SHOES.

THE LADY THEN BURST INTO TEARS AND WITH A SHIVERING VOICE TOLD ME THAT SHE HAS BEEN DOING THIS EVERY MORNING FOR THE PAST 60 YEARS IN THE HOPE THAT SHE CAN HELP SFISO CROSSOVER BUT WITH NO LUCK. WHEN SHE WAKES UP EVERY MORNING THE SHOES APPEAR BESIDE HER SON:S BED.

SHE SPEAKS AND PRAYS TO THE SHOES EVERY MORNING AND AT MIDNIGHT SO THAT THE MOTHERS OF THE DECEASED SONS WHO COULD NOT BURY THEIR CHILDREN WOULD NOT SUFFER THE SAME FATE SHE DID.

THE WOMEN OF NDLOVU HAVE SINCE STARTED A TRADITION OF SOMEWHAT HELPING SFISO MAKE HIS TRANSITION BY ALSO HANGING

A PAIR OF SHOES TO ANY STREET CABLE THAT THEY FIND IN THE MORNING. THIS HAS INSPIRED MOTHERS OR SIBLINGS OF DECEASED BROTHERS AND SONS FROM MANY TOWNSHIPS IN THE COUNTRY.

"I AM BOUND BY THIS TRAGEDY". SHE SAID...

"MY MOTHER'S SHOES CAME WITH A PRICE". SHE UTTERED...

AND NOW I COME TO YOU FOR HELP TO SET ME FREE FROM THIS CURSE, SO I CAN DIE IN PEACE.

I PITIED THIS WOMAN. SO I SPOKE TO MOYA DEEP INSIDE ME AND PRAYED FOR THE GLASS OF WATER NEXT TO HER. SHE DRANK THE WATER AND THANKED ME FOR IT.

THE REST I WILL TELL YOU WHEN I SEE YOU MKHULU. SHOES ARE VERY SPIRITUALLY INTENSE OBJECTS. BUT THIS COULD ALSO TEACH US WHICH PATHS PEOPLE CHOOSE FOR THEIR OFFSPRING. SFISO COULD HAVE SUCCEEDED WITHOUT THE MUTI. THANK GOD IT ENDED, MAY HIS SOUL DANCE IN PEACE.

SINCERELY, YOU'RE INITIATE

"Man Know Thyself, And Ye Shall Know God' - Ancient Egyptian Proverb

Dream Diary Entry

Dream Title:

____

What was the dream about?

____

____

____

____

____

Where it took place:

____

____

____

____

____

My interpretation:

____

____

____

Keywords/phrases spoken within the dream:

Dream symbols:

Note to Self:

Azanian T

By Frederick Masonga, February 18, 2008

Which came first – the spe

A woman's eggs could influence the likelihood to conceive with a particular partner by releasing attachment chemicals that can absorb more sperm from some individuals than others. Only a tiny amount of sperm fluid reaches the egg after sexual intercourse. Professor Dumisani Mshishi from the Fertility unit at the University of Africology says that this phenomena has only been described in humans. The 3rd year fertility and reproductive health graduate body have studied DNA samples from tests on sperm and follicular fluids – this nourishing fluid surrounds an egg while in development and when it is released. These findings were collected from 17 couples undergoing fertility treatments. Sperm travels through follicular fluid on its way to reach an egg for fertilization. Researchers have discovered that the female follicular fluid attracts more sperm from some males than others.

Azanian Ti

By Nondumiso Mthembu, March 8, 2008

Mysterious Typhoon Devas

The Philippine government has ordered their main airport to close after a massive typhoon hit the countries capital from the eastern winds on Saturday morning. 2 million people have been evacuated and medical authorities were sent to assist. The economic hub of the nation (Manila) was greatly affected as the typhoon killed 20 people and also causing a premature volcanic eruption resulting in mudflows which covered at least 250 houses before exiting for the south pacific. Typhoon Oguuni has left many citizens destitute and without any food or shelter for the past week while it continues to cross and make its way to japan. Geologists are predicting that the typhoon came from the Middle East and gathered momentum as it crossed through the Silk Road aiming towards the Far East. In more than three other states residents were trapped by the raging mudflows in the community and coupled with downed communication, made it hard for people to contact each other.

CHAPTER 2

GWABABA: AFRICAN ORIGINS OF APPROACH ANXIETY

DEAR MKHULU,

I WAS AT A WEDDING ON SATURDAY LAST WEEK AND WANTED TO SHARE THIS ANECDOTE WITH YOU. THE MAN WHO SHARED THIS STORY WITH US MIGHT HAVE LIED TO US, BUT ANYWAY A STORY IS A STORY NONETHELESS. THE TALE HAS MISSING PIECES AS I WAS NOT PAYING ATTENTION THAT MUCH BECAUSE I WAS INVITED TO PRAY FOR THE GROOM AND WAS NOT FOCUSED ENOUGH TO GATHER ALL THE TINY DETAILS. I WANT TO TELL YOU THIS STORY SO THAT WE CAN HAVE AN IMPORTANT CONVERSATION AFTERWARD.

FROM WHAT I COULD UNDERSTAND, THIS STORY ADDRESSES MALE AND FEMALE INSECURITY AS IT PERTAINS TO THE SEXUAL DOMINANCE HIERARCHY IN AN AFRICAN CONTEXT. WHAT SEEMS LIKE AN AFRICAN ALLEGORY PAINTS A CANVAS ABOUT WHY SOME MEN IN THE 21ST CENTURY FIND IT DIFFICULT TO SUCCESSFULLY APPROACH AND CONDUCT HEALTHY RELATIONSHIPS WITH WOMEN WHO THEY FIND ATTRACTIVE.

THE MYTH TAKES PLACE HUNDREDS OF YEARS AGO BETWEEN THE BORDERS OF WHAT IS TODAY MODERN-DAY ZIMBABWE AND SOUTH AFRICA. THE SMALL KINGDOM OF NAMMA IS SITUATED IN THIS

DEEPLY TROPICAL REGION OF SOUTHERN AFRICA AND IS RUN BY EMPEROR KANANDA AND HIS WELL-RESPECTED FAMILY.

AT THIS TIME, THE AFRICAN CONTINENT WAS LUSH WITH A GREEN LANDSCAPE OF VEGETATION AND A PICTURESQUE GLOW OF WILDLIFE AND BEAUTIFUL PEOPLE. THERE WAS NOTHING THAT THE PEOPLE OF SOUTHERN AFRICA DID NOT HAVE.

THE PEOPLE LIVED IN PEACE AND HARMONY TOGETHER WITH THE BLOSSOMING BIODIVERSITY THAT THE CREATOR PROVIDED FOR THEM. THIS SMALL KINGDOM BLESSED IN ITS SPLENDOUR BECAME NO STRANGER TO MYSTERY AND MAGIC. HIS EXCELLENCY EMPEROR KANANDA, A MAN OF GREAT WEALTH AND ESTEEM RESPECTED BY HIS PEERS AND FEARED BY HIS ENEMIES RECEIVES ANOTHER BLESSING FROM THE CREATOR AS HIS 3RD WIFE GIVES BIRTH TO TRIPLETS ON A GORGEOUS FULL MOON ON A HOT SUMMER NIGHT IN NAMMA.

A MAN WITH NO HEIR TO HIS NAME BECOMES A FATHER TO THREE DAUGHTERS THAT DAY. LITTLE DID HE KNOW THAT THESE THREE DAUGHTERS WOULD ALTER THE COURSE OF EASTERN HUMAN EVOLUTION AND WOULD SET A CHAIN OF EVENTS INTO PLACE, COMPLETELY SHIFTING OUR PERCEPTION OF REALITY INTO ANCIENT SPIRITUAL FOLKLORE...?

QUEEN PAKHO, AS GORGEOUS AS SHE WAS, WOULD RAISE THE

THREE GIRLS INTO BEAUTIFUL TALL WOMEN, WITH SKIN DARK AND EYES CAT-LIKE WITH PUPILS THAT LOOKED LIKE THE SOUTHERN AFRICAN STARS. EACH GIRL BEAUTIFUL THAN THE NEXT AND EACH ONE WITH HER FLAWS AND SHORTCOMINGS.

THE TRIPLETS WHOSE NAMES GO BY OSHWI, OYA, AND OBWA LOVED THEIR PEOPLE AND CHERISHED THEIR PARENTS DEEPLY. EACH WITH A UNIQUE TALENT AND NOTORIOUSNESS OF SKILL WITH A DASH OF PHYSICAL PERFECTION THEY BECAME ICONS.

OSHWI WAS A VERY CALM AND POLITE WOMAN, WHOSE LOVE FOR FASHION MADE HER ONE OF THE MOST ENVIED WOMEN OF HER TIME AS SHE COULD DESIGN AND MAKE OUTFITS THAT COULD MAKE FLOWERS SHY.

OYA WITH HER ENTICING SMILE WAS AN INTENSELY PASSIONATE WOMAN, WHO COULD MIX EXOTIC BERRIES AND OILS TO CREATE MAKEUP THAT MADE HER DIMPLES STAND OUT AND EVEN CAUSED A SOOTHING RAIN WHEN SHE APPEARED OUTSIDE THE CASTLE ON THE SABBATH.

AND LASTLY OBWA A WOMAN WHO BROKE NECKS WHEN SHE MOVED HER BODY COULD HEAL THE SICK WITH HER ENCHANTING BODY MOVEMENTS AND INSPIRE ACTION IN MEN WITH HER FAMOUS HYPNOTIC GODDESS STARE.

THESE THREE WOMEN HAD IT ALL; RICHES, BEAUTY, AND TALENT. BUT ALL THREE STILL YEARNED FOR SOMETHING THAT ONLY AN EMPRESS COULD HAVE "THE POWER TO COMMAND A NATION".

A WISE MAN ONCE TOLD ME THAT WITH PRIVILEGE COMES GREED. THIS NEED FOR POWER WOULD OPEN UP DESPERATION AND LEAD TO CONFLICT SOON.

AS THE DAUGHTERS GREW IN BEAUTY, SO DID THE KINGDOM OF NAMMA AS A MILITARY GIANT – TERRITORIAL SPACE GREW, AND THE NOTORIETY OF THEIR DYNASTY UNMATCHED. AT THE END OF THE GREAT WARS OF MUTAPA, THE KING WAS OLD AND THE QUEEN LATER PASSED AWAY DUE TO LEPROSY ON HER VISIT TO THE NAPA LANDS IN THE NEAR NORTH-EASTERN PROVINCE.

WHEN THESE TRAGIC DEATHS CLOAKED THE EMPIRE THE FIRST INSTRUCTION FROM THE QUEEN WAS FOR THE KINGS' VIZIER TO VISIT THE PRINCESSES EACH AT THEIR PALACES.

HE TOLD THEM ABOUT THE PROPHECY OF THE GREAT SON OF THE NORTH WHO WAS VISITED BY AN ORACLE AS A TEENAGER AND WAS TOLD THAT HE WOULD UNITE THE FEUDAL LANDS FROM ACROSS THE GREAT LAKES THROUGH MARRIAGE WITH A DAUGHTER DESCENDING FROM THE LINE OF THE LAST EMPEROR OF NAMMA SO THAT THE SOUTHERN AFRICAN KINGDOMS CAN PRODUCE THE FINEST WARRIORS OUT OF THEIR UNION. A POWERFUL AND PRESTIGIOUS LEGACY THAT

WOULD WITHER THE SANDS OF TIME. THE VIZIER THEN ACCLAIMED THAT THE CHOSEN DAUGHTER WILL BE GIVEN A MAGICAL MIRROR MADE FROM THE NAMMA MOUNTAIN CRYSTAL, AND THIS WOULD GRANT THE QUEEN WITH ETERNAL YOUTH AND ADORNMENT FOREVER AND EVER. THE VIZIER LEFT AND COULD NOT DISCLOSE MORE ABOUT THE SUBJECT AS HE WAS ONLY TOLD WHAT TO SAY READING FROM THE ROYAL SCROLL.

A YEAR PASSED AND THE DAUGHTERS RAN THEIR INHERITED KINGDOM AS BEST AS THEY COULD. WAR AFTER WAR THEIR KINGDOMS' TERRITORIAL SPACE SHRUNK AND THEIR STATUS BEGAN TO DIMINISH. IN A FRIGHTENING ATTEMPT TO UNDERSTAND THEIR CIRCUMSTANCES, THEY SENT POWERFUL MYSTICS ACROSS THE SOUTHERN RIVERS AND MOUNTAINS TO LOOK FOR THE GREAT SON AND A WEAPON THAT COULD HELP THEIR ARMY IN BATTLE.

8 MONTHS PASSED AND THE SOUTHERN MYSTICS RETURNED TO THE KINGDOM WITH NEWS OF A GREAT EMPEROR FROM THE NORTH APPROACHING THE SOUTH WITH A FLEET OF 200 CAMELS AND 300 ELEPHANTS OF WHICH ARE ALL CARRYING GOLD, RUBIES, EXOTIC SPICES, AND FABRICS FOR A QUEEN IN THE SOUTHERN MOUNTAINS.

THE MYSTICS SAID THAT THE EMPEROR ALSO HOLDS A CHEST WITH AN OBJECT THAT COULD DO MIRACLES BEFORE THE GODS. BEFORE THE QUEENS COULD ASK QUESTIONS THE MYSTICS BROUGHT FORTH A MAN COVERED IN A DARK VIOLET HOODED CLOAK HOLDING A STAFF

AND WALKING TOWARDS THE THRONES WITH A SLIGHT LIMP.

"WHO IS THIS MAN," SAID THE SISTERS...

"IT IS THE SUPREME SAMU OF SOUTHERN AFRICA, AND HE HOLDS SECRETS FOR EACH ONE OF YOU", SAID THE MYSTICS PROFUSELY...

"LET HIM SPEAK", SAID THE QUEENS...

THE SAMU HAD IMPORTANT INFORMATION TO TELL THE SISTERS AND THAT THIS INFORMATION WAS NOT TO BE SHARED OR DISCUSSED BETWEEN EACH OTHER. THE SAMU ADDED THAT HE COULD HELP THEM GAIN THEIR STRENGTH AS A NATION AND THAT HE POSSESSES THE POWER OF MOYA.

HE DISPLAYED HIS POWER AND GAINED THE TRUST OF THE SISTERS DURING THE THREE WEEKS THAT HE WAS AT THE KINGDOM. THE SAMU VISITED THE QUEENS INDIVIDUALLY AND REVEALED SOMETHING THAT WOULD INSTANTLY CHANGE THEIR RELATIONSHIP WITH EACH OTHER.

"INDEED YOU ARE BEAUTIFUL AND TALENTED, BUT FOR YOU TO BE CHOSEN BY THE EMPEROR YOU NEED THE POWER OF THE NTHATE PLANT", HE SUGGESTED...

ALL THREE OF THEM WITH CURIOSITY ASKED THE MYSTIC WHAT HE WAS IMPLYING AND ALL WERE TOLD ABOUT THE NTHATE PLANT,

WHICH IS A RED FLOWER WITH A FIERY SEED INSIDE ITS PATEL'S THAT HAD SUPERNATURAL POWERS. THIS PLANT CAN EITHER BE COOKED OR CAN BE BATHED AT MIDNIGHT WITH SOUTHERN AFRICAN SEAWATER. WHEN COOKED FOR A MAN IN A STEW, THE MAN WILL FALL IN LOVE WITH A WOMAN AND WORSHIP HER.

BUT IF THE PLANT IS EXPOSED TO THE SUN IT WILL TURN MEN IN THE KINGDOM INTO PERVERTS THAT WILL LUST FOR SEX UNTIL THE DAWN OF TIME.

NOT PAYING ATTENTION TO THE SAMU, THE SISTERS ALL STARRED AT THE PLANT AND EACH THOUGHT WHAT POWER THEY WOULD WIELD IF THEY COULD HARNESS THE PLANT INTO THEIR UNIQUE TALENTS.

THE SISTERS EACH STAYED WITHIN THE CONFINES OF THEIR CASTLES AND PLANNED THEIR SEDUCTIVE STRATEGIES TO A TEA - DAY IN AND DAY OUT. 5 WEEKS PASSED AND NEWS OF THE GREAT EMPEROR CLOSED WITHIN THE WALLS OF THE KINGDOM. A ROYAL ENTOURAGE OF PRIESTS ENTERED THE KINGDOMS' ROYAL COURTS AND MADE THEIR WAY TO THE PALACE.

AS THE MYSTERIOUS EMPEROR CLIMBED OUT OF HIS CHARIOT A TEMPORARY THRONE WAS ERECTED FOR HIM TO SIT AND AWAIT THE PRESENCE OF THE THREE QUEENS FOR A FORMAL GREETING TO TAKE PLACE BETWEEN THE TWO CULTURES.

OSHWI CAME OUT THE FIRST AND HAD SECRETLY WOVEN THE NTHATE PLANT INTO HER SUMMER DRES'S GOWN. SHE WALKED TOWARDS THE THRONE AND INTRODUCED HERSELF. THEN OYA APPEARED FROM THE LEFT AND DAZZLED THE CROWD WITH MAKEUP THAT CONSISTED OF THE AROMA OF THE PLANT ON HER FACE.

AND LASTLY, OBWA APPROACHED THE THRONE TO HER RIGHT AND STRUTTED A POWERFUL WALK WITH THE PLANT PLACED IN HER UNDERWEAR AROUND HER WAIST. THIS EVENT WAS THE MOST MAGNIFICENT SPECTACLE EVER SEEN AND LEFT ALL THE MEN IN AWE.

TRUTH OR MYTH

In early roman societies, certain aromas of perfume were used by Wiccans as aphrodisiacs. The smell of chocolate was one of them.

THE ENERGY OF THE PLANT WAS SO STRONG THAT THE EMPEROR FROZE IN SHOCK AND ITS MAGNETIC CURRENT PUT THE GUESTS IN A DEEP MELLOW TRANCE.

IT WAS LATER REVEALED THAT THE NTHATE PLANT BECAME HIGHLY POISONOUS AFTER BEING UPROOTED FOR DAYS AND THE EMPERORS' REASON FOR COMING TO NAMMA WAS TO ALSO SEEK MEDICAL CURES FOR HIS ALLERGIC REACTION TO WILD PLANTS. THE EMPEROR TRIED TO STAND UP BUT COLLAPSED AT THE FEET OF THE QUEENS' GOWNS. THE TALE HAS MANY ENDINGS BUT WHAT I WAS TOLD WAS THAT THE KING SUFFERED A STRANGE HEART ATTACK AND DIED ON THE SPOT.

THE QUEENS WERE NOT EVEN PAYING ATTENTION BECAUSE THEY WERE BEING PRAISED FOR THEIR BEAUTY AT THAT MOMENT AND VANITY KICKED IN.

TO CUT A LONG STORY SHORT, MANDLA (THE GROOMS' BEST MAN) CONCLUDED THE STORY BY EXPLAINING THAT THE PLANT WAS EXPOSED TO THE SUN FOR SO LONG AND LOST ITS EARTHLY SUSTENANCE FROM BEING UPROOTED FOR DAYS WHICH CAUSED THE SISTERS TO GET INTOXICATED BY THEIR BEAUTY. THIS PLANT TURNED THEM INTO NARCISSISTS AND MADE THEM FALL IN LOVE WITH THEMSELVES INSTEAD. THE EMPERORS' ALLERGIC REACTION CLOSED HIS NASAL PASSAGES FROM INSIDE AND ALSO DEVELOPED A BURNING SENSATION IN HIS CHEST CAUSING A HEART ATTACK.

THIS SENSATION HAS LINGERED FOR CENTURIES TO COME BECAUSE OF THE UNRESTED SPIRIT OF THE EMPEROR WHICH CULMINATED INTO A SPIRIT, FEEDING OFF THE ENERGY OF MEN AND WOMEN FOR GENERATIONS TO COME.

SO I BOLDLY ASKED MANDLA BEFORE WE LEFT THE WEDDING VENUE, COULD IT BE THAT THE MALE DESCENDANTS OF THE NAMMA TRIBE EXPERIENCE GWABABA TODAY BECAUSE THE SPIRIT OF THE NTHATE PLANT BURNS THEM FROM WITHIN?

HE LAUGHED AND COULDN'T ANSWER ME...

MKHULU, DO YOU THINK THAT OSHWI, OYA, AND OBWA WERE USING THE SAMU'S MOYA TO SUBCONSCIOUSLY COMPETE WITH EACH OTHER FOR ATTENTION?

IS THIS THE REASON WHY MEN ARE ALWAYS CHEATING ON THEIR WIVES IN RELATIONSHIPS BECAUSE THEY HAVE BEEN DEEPLY SEDUCED BY THE REVEALING LINGERIE, THE SEDUCTIVE MAKEUP, AND THE HYPNOTIC EYES AND HIPS OF OTHER WOMEN WHO COULD BE USING LOVE POTIONS?

WE WILL NEVER KNOW, I GUESS.

HOPE YOU WRITE BACK.

SINCERELY, YOU'RE INITIATE

''People Change but God Never Does'' - Thabang H.A Mathapo

Dream Diary Entry

Dream Title:

____

What was the dream about?

____

____

____

____

____

Where it took place:

____

____

____

____

____

My interpretation:

____

____

____

Keywords/phrases spoken within the dream:

Dream symbols:

Note to Self:

Azanian Ti

By Busisiwe Khoza, March 12, 2008

Hill of Persia's Past

In a forgotten piece of vast land in the outskirts of Iran lies an unrested spirit. Today lies an abandoned army post in its surrounding area where a story of a cursed village near Taliban insurgents reside. This vacated outpost has flagged itself in both American and local Persian culture as part of an urban legend. It is the backdrop for a ghost story built along the sand dunes of Iran's past and present wars and its relationship with the unburied dead. For the past 1000 years there have not been proper burial practices amongst the locals and so unrested spirits hover across the desert and eat away at the Taliban men as they cross the land. The Taliban roam freely among the clusters of small villages and poppy fields, of which some are irrigated by a canal system built during the Cold War and funded by the United States. This has led to a resurgence of more ghosts that feed of the desperation and hunger of the village dwellers as there has been a shortage of crops since last year's drought.

Azanian T

By Rethabile Ncube, March 16, 2008

Nigerian Man has 90 wives

Adonyjah Mansa is a controversial patriarch in the small village of Budu, Ogun state, where he has married more than 200 women. He is hailed as West Africa's most famous polygamist and shows no sign of stopping anytime soon. The 95 year old Nigerian man has no stable income, and has conflicted with the Islamic elders in his hometown, who some have accused him of running a brothel. Mr Mansa has fathered over 185 children that we know of and has told Azanian Times reporters that he faces ridicule from the government as the state is liable to provide welfare to the descendants of a non-taxpayer. When asked about his fertility he said the creator once spoke to him, saying from him there will be a nation born of kings that will usher in a renaissance of knowledge and wisdom. He continued by saying he has a heavenly assignment given to him from his ancestors directly from god and he will keep planting seeds till the end. Mr Mansa has married a total of 108 women in his time,

CHAPTER 3

LAST TRAIN FROM EXTENSION SIX

DEAR MKHULU,

BEFORE I FORGET I WOULD LIKE TO TELL YOU A STORY. A STORY ABOUT A MAN, HIS SON, AND A VERY UNUSUAL EVENT. THIS STORY MAY HAVE STARTED DECADES AGO AND COULD NOT HAVE ENDED AS I WRITE YOU THIS SHORT LETTER. YOU WERE CORRECT ABOUT SPIRITS INHIBITING MECHANICAL OBJECTS BECAUSE MACHINES ARE MOVING MECHANISMS. I GUESS YOU COULD HAVE ALSO HEARD ABOUT A MYSTERIOUS TRAIN MAKING HEADLINES AS OF LATE.

THERE SEEMS TO BE A SECRET ABOUT A PARTICULAR TRAIN, WHICH SEEMS TO BE ABDUCTING THE YOUNG POPULATION OF THE AREA YOU ONCE TOLD ME ABOUT.

THIS LOCATION IS 2KM BEFORE THE HARTEBEESPOORT DAM AND IS THE HOME TO MANY STRUGGLE HEROES OF OUR NATION.

THIS SMALL NEGLECTED TOWNSHIP WHICH WAS ONCE A SUBURB IS CALLED INDABA AND IS MADE UP OF 2 DISTRICTS TODAY. THEY ARE DIVIDED INTO EXTENSIONS 1 – 3 AND EXTENSIONS 4 – 6. A LOT HAS CHANGED SINCE YOU HAVE BEEN THERE, THE ENVIRONMENT HAS COMPLETELY TURNED INTO A DECAYING TOWNSHIP.

INDABA IS NOW RIFE WITH A LACK OF ECONOMIC OPPORTUNITIES FOR THE RESIDENTS IN THAT REGION, GIVING RISE TO A HIGH CRIME RATE, DILAPIDATED INFRASTRUCTURE, AND A DISASTROUS DECAY OF POLITICAL WILL BY ITS COMMUNITY LEADERS.

IT'S EVERY MAN FOR HIMSELF AND HIS FAMILY. A LIFESTYLE THAT MANY HAVE ADOPTED BUT THIS DOES NOT STOP MR STEVE ZULU FROM BEING OPTIMISTIC AND PROVIDING FOR HIS FAMILY. STEVE AKA BRA STEVE, IS A SECURITY GUARD AT THE INDABA TRAIN STATION AND HAS BEEN WORKING THERE FOR THE PAST 17 YEARS.

A STRUGGLING VETERAN WHO SUFFERS FROM POST-TRAUMATIC STRESS AND ANXIETY FROM AN AGE OF FREEDOM FIGHTING WROTE TO ME TELLING ME THAT HE SOMETIMES LOSES HIS EYESIGHT AND HEARS VOICES IN HIS HEAD IN THE MORNING.

BRA STEVE SEEMED TO BE A HARD-WORKING FAMILY MAN WITH A WIFE AND SON WHO SUPPORT AND LOVE EACH OTHER.

BRA STEVE ALWAYS STRESSED HOW HE WISHED TO RETIRE AFTER 3 YEARS, SO HE CAN OBTAIN A MATURE PENSION WITH MEDICAL BENEFITS, AS HE IS STARTING TO EXPERIENCE AN EXCRUCIATING SPINAL ACHE WHICH MAKES IT DIFFICULT FOR HIM TO STAND AND WALK FOR LONG PERIODS AT THE STATION.

HIS JOB HAS TAKEN A TOLL ON HIM PLUS HE WISHED TO RETIRE SO

HE COULD DEDICATE MORE TIME IN RAISING HIS SON.

WHAT CAUGHT MY ATTENTION IS THAT THE LETTER HE WROTE TO ME WAS WRINKLED. WHEN I FOUND THE ENVELOPE UNDER THE DOOR WHEN I ARRIVED HOME FROM WORK THE PAGES WERE DIRTY WHICH SUGGESTED THAT HE WAS CRYING WHEN HE WROTE IT. MOYA TELLS ME THAT BRA STEVE HAS BEEN SHAKEN AND THE THINGS THAT HE HAS EXPERIENCED IN HIS LIFE WERE PARTLY DUE TO HIS SPIRITUAL TRAUMA OF WHAT HAPPENED DURING THE HECTIC YEARS OF THE APARTHEID STRUGGLE AT INDABA. SINCE THEN HE HAS LOST FAMILY, RELATIVES AND HAS DEVELOPED PHYSICAL PAIN FROM THE SPIRITS ATTACHED TO HIS STRESS.

HE NEEDED TO GO TO A PROPHET FOR A PROPER BAPTISMAL CLEANSING TO RID HIMSELF OF THE NEGATIVE ENERGY ATTACHED TO HIS MIND. BUT BEFORE I CONTINUE ABOUT HIS AILMENTS, LET ME FIRST EXPLAIN WHAT CAUSED THEM.

A COUPLE OF MONTHS AGO, BRA STEVE AND HIS SON "ISAAC" WERE VISITING A FELLOW NEIGHBOURS' HOUSE AT EXTENSION 4. AT THIS HOUSE, ISAAC MET A GROUP OF YOUNG BOYS WHO REVEALED THEMSELVES TO BE TRAIN SURFERS. YOU MIGHT WONDER WHAT TRAIN SURFING IS BUT I WILL EXPLAIN WHEN I SEE YOU AGAIN. THE LEADER OF THIS GROUP WAS CALLED LUCAS AND HE AND ISAAC BECAME FRIENDS INSTANTLY OVER THAT SHORT PERIOD OF A WEEKEND.

BRA STEVE MAKES IT CLEAR IN HIS NOTE, THAT HE WARNED ISAAC ABOUT THE KIDS FROM EXTENSION 4.

THE COMMUNITY NEWSPAPER OF INDABA HAS ARTICLES ON THE CRIMINAL ALLEGATIONS AMONGST THE YOUNG PEOPLE OF EXTENSION 4. INFLUENCED BY PEER PRESSURE, ISAAC GAVE INTO THE BAD HABITS OF HIS BEST FRIEND AND WAS NOW SWALLOWED BY THE WORLD OF DRUGS, TRAIN SURFING, MUGGING, AND VANDALISM.

I THOUGHT THAT BRA STEVE COULD HAVE BEEN EXAGGERATING A BIT SINCE MANY KIDS ABOVE 15 GO THROUGH A PHASE BUT WHAT HE DISCLOSED NEXT, GOT ME WORRIED ABOUT THE LIVES OF YOUNG PEOPLE IN INDABA.

I HAVE COME TO REALIZE THAT THERE IS A FINE LINE BETWEEN ADOLESCENT BEHAVIOUR AND IRRATIONAL IRRESPONSIBILITY.

TRUTH OR MYTH

The Berber people travel on camelback because camels possess superior navigational prowess.

BRA STEVE'S LETTER TO ME WAS NOT ABOUT HELPING HIM WITH HIS BODILY IMPEDIMENTS OR CHANNELING THE POWER OF MOYA TO REVIVE HIS SON FROM HIS LACK OF DIRECTION.

THIS GETS INTERESTING, MKHULU...

HE SAID HE FEARED FOR HIS SONS' LIFE BECAUSE HE GOES TO SCHOOL IN THE MORNING BUT COMES HOME AFTER MIDNIGHT SOMETIMES. HE MENTIONED A PHENOMENON CALLED THE LAST TRAIN FROM EXTENSION SIX WHICH HE EXCLAIMED AS A CURSE CLOUDING THEIR NEIGHBOURHOOD WHERE THEY ARE CURRENTLY RESIDING TODAY.

HE LATER ADMITS TO A NEED FOR CLEANSING IS BECAUSE HE THINKS THAT HE MIGHT BE PUTTING HIS SON AND MAYBE HIS WIFE'S LIFE IN DANGER BASED ON A SUPERNATURAL EVENT THAT TOOK PLACE IN 1987 WHEN A TRAIN WENT MISSING DURING THE INDABA UPRISING. THIS ICONIC STUDENT PROTEST WAS INITIATED BY VERNON DABELE, WHO AT THAT TIME WAS A TRAIN CONDUCTOR WORKING FOR THE THEN KRUGER TRAIN STATION – VAN ZUID AFRIKA.

THIS MYSTERIOUS EVENT INVOLVES VERNON'S SACRIFICE AND DESPERATION TO AVENGE THE MURDER OF HIS 12-YEAR-OLD DAUGHTER AT THE TIME. CIVIL UNREST WAS FOUGHT AND WON BY THE RESIDENTS OF INDABA BUT IT CAME AT A PRICE.

BEAR IN MIND THAT ONLY A FEW PEOPLE KNOW ABOUT THIS MKHULU...

BRA STEVE THEN EXPLAINS THAT TO PROTECT THE SCHOOL KIDS OF INDABA AND TO OVERTHROW THE APARTHEID POLICE, A RITUAL WAS PERFORMED BY VERNON'S AUNT ON THE TRAIN SO THAT WHEN THE TRAIN PASSES AT MIDNIGHT OR 03:00 AM AN ENTITY BY THE NAME OF GYLO WOULD SLAY THE POLICE USING AN ELECTRIFIED COPPER WIRE. HE CLARIFIED THAT THE PRICE TO BE PAID BY THE INDABA PEOPLE WOULD BE FOR THE TRAIN SPIRIT TO ALSO TAKE AN INNOCENT SOUL NOW AND THEN TO BALANCE ITS KARMA.

VERNON WAS BRUTALLY MURDERED BEFORE THE REVOLUTION ENDED, AND SO THE SPELL BECAME A CURSE AND ATTACHED TO HIS SPIRIT.

BRA STEVE SAID THAT HE HEARD ABOUT THIS FROM THE FRIEND THEY WERE VISITING THE DAY ISAAC MET LUCAS. LUCAS IS A RELATIVE TO VERNON'S AUNT, WHO MOVED TO THE EASTERN CAPE DECADES AGO. BRA STEVE IS AFRAID FOR HIS SON'S LIFE BECAUSE HE SAID HE WAS ALSO INVOLVED IN THE UPRISING AND HAS BEEN WORKING AT THE SAME STATION WHICH VERNON WORKED AT. HE BELIEVES THIS COULD AFFECT HIM AND HIS SON IN THE FUTURE IF I DO NOT INTERVENE WITH THE FORCES OF MOYA.

HE ENDED BY PLEADING FOR HELP FOR THE POWER OF MOYA FROM US ESPECIALLY EVEN MORE SINCE THE BEGINNING OF LAST MONTH LUCAS WENT MISSING AT NIGHT AND HAS NOT BEEN FOUND YET.

AUTHORITIES SAY IT MIGHT HAVE BEEN A DRUG WAR, BUT SOME COMMUNITY MEMBERS THINK THERE COULD BE WITCHCRAFT INVOLVED. WHEN I EXAMINE THIS CASE USING THE WATER RITUAL AND THE POWER OF MOYA, I CAN SEE THAT ONLY THE SURVIVORS OF THE 1987 UPRISING CAN HEAR THE TRAIN AT NIGHT AND DECIDE TO KEEP IT A SECRET AMONGST THEM.

MOYA TELLS ME THAT THE TRAIN PASSES THROUGH EVERY STREET AND A SHARP BANG OF STEEL CAN BE HEARD INSIDE OF IT. THIS IS THE ENTITY INSIDE THE TRAIN PREPARING ITS WEAPON TO SLAY THE INNOCENT SOUL OF WHICH IT NEEDS FOR ENERGY.

I WILL HELP BRA STEVE, BUT THIS WILL REQUIRE THAT I FACE THE TRAIN SPIRIT ALONE AT NIGHT WITH YOU.

PLEASE UNDERSTAND MKHULU, THESE PEOPLE NEED US.

LAST NIGHT AFTER READING STEVE'S LETTER, I COULD HEAR THE TRAIN PASSING THROUGH THE STREET OF INDABA WITH THE VOICES OF THE INNOCENT CHILDREN SCREAMING FOR HELP IN MY DREAM.

SINCERELY, YOU'E INITIATE

''Even A Useless Man Is Useful'-

- Thabang H.A Mathapo

Dream Diary Entry

Dream Title:

____

What was the dream about?

____

____

____

____

____

Where it took place:

____

____

____

____

____

My interpretation:

____

____

____

Keywords/phrases spoken within the dream:

Dream symbols:

Note to Self:

Azanian Ti

By Nicholas Sadat, March 25, 2008

Secluded Island Tribe Kill

A body of a man who kayaked to an island full of isolated indigenous people was recovered offshore by maritime coast guards. The tribe of remote Indians impaled the man by shooting him with bows and arrows. Jack Prince, 27, was identified as the victim by Stacey Beckham, a secretary of the missionary of Christ foundation. Prince had written a post about his interactions with Stacey prior his death about him going on an expedition alone. Prince's mission was to evangelize Christianity by bringing his religious beliefs to remote indigenous tribes of African descent. His perception of people who do not possess the same belief system that he does is that they have to be saved from their misery. The Sentinelese people are resistant to foreigners and often attack anyone who comes near, and visits to the island are heavily restricted by the government. Prince knew what he was getting himself into by approaching the Sentinelese people. He was raised in a euro centric Christian family and was told by his community

Azanian T

By Fezile Mantashe, March 28, 2008

My Husband the Bug

One man in a small town of QwaQwa has taken social media by storm. In a video clip that recently surfaced across multiple platforms has amazed South Africans. A man who until now remains unnamed has been exposed by his wife for displaying strange behaviour since coming back from their honey moon last winter. The woman explained that her husband is a successful actor who has worked alongside many A-list celebrities in a number of films locally. But as a result of the retrenchment he faced after arriving back from Mauritius, he hasn't had any work. One morning she woke up and found her husband on the floor behaving weirdly like an insect. He was crawling on all fours and chasing insects around the yard. At first she thought he was joking around but after a couple of hours she noticed a shift in his psychology. Her husband had soiled himself and had lost control of his bowels.

CHAPTER 4

SPIRITUAL HUSBANDS

DEAR MKHULU,

AS I SCROLL THROUGH MY EMAILS THIS MORNING I AM BEGINNING TO SEE A DISTURBING TREND. MOST OF THE FEMALE CLIENTS WHO HAVE SENT ME AN EMAIL SEEM TO BE EXPERIENCING THE SAME DILEMMA. I REMEMBER YOU TELLING ME AFTER MY INITIATION THAT SPIRITS ARE OFTEN CREATED BY AN INTENSE EMOTION WHEN A GROUP OF PEOPLE DESIRE SIMILAR OBJECTIVES. WITH THAT BEING SAID, WOMEN ARE EXTREMELY POWERFUL AND CAN BRING FORTH ENTITIES IN PHYSICAL FORM OR BE ABLE TO CONJURE SPIRITS TO PERFORM CERTAIN TASKS.

MEN, ON THE OTHER HAND, ARE ALSO POWERFUL BUT THEIR POWER COMES FROM CREATING SPIRITS TO MANIPULATE THE UNSEEN FORCES OF THE UNIVERSE. WE ARE NOW AT A POINT IN OUR SOCIETY WHERE WE ARE DELVING INTO THE ESOTERIC MYSTICISM OF THE AGGREGORE SPIRIT.

AN ENTITY THAT FEEDS ON LARGE GROUP-BASED IDEOLOGIES OR BELIEF SYSTEMS.

MKHULU, YOU WERE RIGHT ABOUT HOW GROUPS OF WOMEN COULD BE ABLE TO INTENSELY FOCUS THEIR ENERGY AROUND A PARTICULAR

IDEA AND BE ABLE TO MANIFEST A COLLECTIVE SPIRITUAL PARADIGM.

THIS TIME WOMEN HAVE A VERY UNIQUE CIRCUMSTANCE. THE WOMEN OF SOUTHERN AFRICA STRUGGLE WITH A MASCULINE SPIRIT CALLED, "THE SPIRITUAL HUSBAND". THE SPIRITUAL HUSBAND HAS ITS ORIGINS IN THE EARLY 70'S WHEN THE WOMEN'S LIBERATION MOVEMENT STARTED. MOST OF THE WOMEN WHO HAVE CONTACTED ME ARE WOMEN OF DIGNIFIED STATURE, BACKGROUND, AND ECONOMIC MEANS.

THEY ARE RESPECTED IN THEIR FIELDS AND ARE ESTABLISHED IN THE CORPORATE WORLD. ABOUT 80% OF THE WOMEN WHO CONTACT ME HAVE A SPIRITUAL HUSBAND ISSUE. THE REST OF THE 20% HAVE OTHER RELATED ISSUES CONCERNING RELATIONSHIPS.

WHAT INTRIGUES ME ABOUT THIS DEBACLE, IS HOW THE WOMEN'S LIBERATION MOVEMENT DEVELOPS INTO WHAT WE KNOW AS FEMINISM AND COMPLETELY GOES TO WAR AGAINST WOMEN WHO CHOSE TO LIVE IN THE TRADITIONAL WOMANIST MANNER.

I BEGAN DOING THE CANDLE WORK THAT YOU TAUGHT ME AND BEGAN MAKING DISCOVERIES DURING MY MANTRA PRACTICES EARLY THIS MORNING.

THIS SPECIFIC ENTITY THAT WE ARE DEALING WITH IS CALLED THE SEX DEMON. THIS ENTITY WAS CREATED BY A SECRET SOCIETY IN

THE LATE 20TH CENTURY WHICH MAINLY CONSISTED OF A GROUP OF INFLUENTIAL WOMEN WHOSE NAMES I DO NOT KNOW.

THIS GROUP OF WOMEN WERE EXTREMELY KNOWLEDGEABLE ABOUT THE ESOTERIC ARTS AND WOULD TRAVEL FROM NORTHERN EUROPE TO CENTRAL AFRICA FOR MYSTIC STUDIES AND BOOKS.

EACH OF THEM HAD A SPECIAL SKILL SET AND DOMINATED A SPECIFIC INDUSTRY IN WORLD AFFAIRS.

WHETHER IN BUSINESS, MEDICINE, OR POLITICS THEY ALL SHARED AN INTEREST IN THE WISE CRAFT OF SPIRITUALITY. THESE EUROPEAN WOMEN WERE ALSO MARRIED TO BANKERS AND FARMERS OF THAT TIME AND HAD CHILDREN WITH THEM.

THIS SECRET CABAL OF WOMEN QUICKLY SPREAD ACROSS THE WESTERN WORLD AND SOON MADE ITSELF THROUGH THE BRITISH COMMUNITIES OF SOUTHERN AND WESTERN AFRICA.

I AM UNABLE TO SEE ANY OF THEIR FACES BY USING MOYA BECAUSE THERE SEEMS TO BE SOMETHING BLOCKING ME FROM ENTERING THIS SPIRITUAL VORTEX.

SOMEWHERE ALONG THE LINE, THE LEADERS OF THIS SECRET SOCIETY BEGAN EXPERIENCING HEARTACHE IN THEIR RELATIONSHIPS.

SOME OF THEM WERE ABUSED BY THEIR HUSBANDS, SOME WERE

CHEATING ON THEIR SPOUSES AND OTHERS WERE SEXUALLY UNSATISFIED WITH THEIR BEDROOM PARTNERS.

WOMEN STARTED CREATING SOCIO-POLITICAL IDEOLOGIES SO THAT THEY COULD CHANGE THE SOCIAL SYSTEM INTO A MATRIARCHAL SOCIETY.

THIS WAS SOMETHING THAT WAS ALSO ENCOURAGED BY A CERTAIN CLASS OF MEN WHO AT THAT TIME WANTED TO USE WOMEN FOR A CERTAIN POLITICAL IDEOLOGY.

WHATEVER THE REASONS WERE THEY ALL AGREED TO CREATE THE EARLY STAGES OF FEMINISM SO THAT THE TRADITIONAL FAMILY STRUCTURE WAS DECONSTRUCTED FOR THEIR PLANS.

THE WOMEN WHO CONTACT ME SAY THAT THEY ARE ALL FEMINISTS AND ARE ON THE FRONTLINES OF THE GENDER POWER STRUGGLE (OR WAR) BETWEEN MEN AND WOMEN.

LITTLE DID THEY KNOW THAT ANY WOMAN WHO TOOK THE OATH OF FEMINISM COULD BE INVITING IN THE SEX DEMON PARASITE IN THEIR LIFE.

THE FEMALE SECRET SOCIETY FROM EUROPE SAW THAT THEIR NUMBERS WERE NOT GROWING RAPIDLY ENOUGH IN THE FIRST YEARS OF THEIR MOVEMENT AND DECIDED TO GATHER ALL THEIR

SACRED AND ESOTERIC KNOWLEDGE FROM ALL OVER THE EASTERN HEMISPHERE SO THEY COULD CREATE AN ENTITY TO ASSIST IN THEIR MISSION.

ON A VERY QUIET WINTER AFTERNOON IN THE CITY OF GOLD (WHAT WE CALL JOHANNESBURG TODAY), THESE WOMEN GATHERED ALL THE POWERFUL OCCULTISTS OF THEIR TIME IN A TEMPLE BUILT AT HILLBROW – JOHANNESBURG, AND CONSTRUCTED A SARCOPHAGUS WHICH THEY PLACED IN THE MIDDLE OF THE HALL. THEY FORMED A CIRCLE AROUND THIS SARCOPHAGUS AND CHANTED MANTRAS USING A MIXTURE OF ARCADIAN, SWAHILI, AND LATIN DIALECTS.

WHEN THEY WERE DONE WITH THE RITUAL ALL THE CANDLES IN THE TEMPLE LIT UP AND ALL THE LIGHTS SWITCHED OFF.

TO THEIR AMUSEMENT, A VOICE WAS HEARD AMONGST THEM SPEAKING IN TONGUES SAYING IT NEEDS ALL THE WOMEN OF THE WORLD TO ITSELF. SINCE THIS WAS SHOCKING TO THEM, THEY SPOKE BACK TO THE SPIRIT AGGRESSIVELY TELLING IT WHAT TO DO FOR THEM.

IT AGREED TO HELP THEM GAIN SOCIAL AND ECONOMIC POWER BUT IT DEMANDED THEM TO LEAVE THEIR HUSBANDS AND HAVE SEX WITH THEM EVERY WEEK. THEY AGREED AND MADE THIS PACT WITH THE DEMON FORGETTING THAT THIS SEX DEMON WAS GOING TO EXIST FOREVER.

THE SECRET SOCIETY THOUGHT THEY COULD CARRY ON WITH THEIR LIVES AND GET REMARRIED AGAIN BUT THE SEX DEMON REFUSED BY CREATING MISHAPS IN THEIR LIVES. SOME OF THEM DIED WITHOUT HAVING CHILDREN AND MOST OF THEM LIVED ALONE UNTIL OLD AGE.

THE SEX DEMON HAD EVOLVED OVER THE DECADES AS A SPIRITUAL HUSBAND AND HAS GROWN STRONGER OVER THE YEARS CREATING DRIFTS BETWEEN MEN AND WOMEN. THE SPIRITUAL HUSBAND HAS BECOME JEALOUS AND ENVIOUS OF MODERN FEMINISTS WHO WANT TO ESTABLISH HOUSEHOLDS WITH MEN.

IT DOES NOT WANT TO SEE A FEMINIST WITH A HUSBAND BECAUSE IT WILL NOT BE ABLE TO EXTRACT SEXUAL POWER FROM A TAKEN WOMAN.

MOST WOMEN OF TODAY MIGHT NOT HAVE INVITED THE SPIRITUAL HUSBAND INTO THEIR LIVES BUT THEY INHERIT THIS SPIRIT THROUGH ITS BELIEFS AND BEHAVIOUR.

MOST OF THESE YOUNG WOMEN WHO ARE CURRENTLY IN A RELATIONSHIP WITH A SPIRITUAL HUSBAND ARE THE ONES WHO HAVE BEEN SENT THIS SPIRIT BY THEIR FEMALE ENEMIES.

WOMEN WHO DABBLE WITH WITCHCRAFT TODAY ARE ALSO ABLE TO CONJURE THIS SPIRIT AND ENGAGE IN SPIRITUAL WARFARE WITH OTHER WOMEN.

TRUTH OR MYTH

Contrary to popular belief women in certain parts of Africa work the land and yield better crops than men.

IN MOST CASES, WOMEN WHO ARE CONNECTED WITH THIS SPIRIT CAN CLEANSE THEMSELVES WITH CERTAIN POTIONS TO RID THEMSELVES OF THIS PARASITE. TODAY THERE SEEMS TO BE MANY AFRICAN WOMEN WHO ARE LIVING WITH SPIRITUAL HUSBANDS AND ARE SUFFERING BECAUSE OF THIS. THESE POOR WOMEN ARE EVEN ADDICTED TO SEX TOYS AND UNHEALTHY FETISHES WHICH THE DEMON HAS CONJURED FOR ITS LONGEVITY ON EARTH.

SINCE THERE ARE SO MANY WOMEN WITH PROBLEMS, PLEASE CAN YOU GIVE ME ADVICE ON HOW TO HELP THEM PERMANENTLY? WE ARE NOW BEGINNING TO SEE THE HARSH REALITY OF THE UNBALANCED GENDER ROLES OF TODAY. I AM NOW SENDING EMAILS TO THESE WOMEN, BUT I WILL WARN AFRICAN WOMEN OF THE NEGATIVE SPIRITUAL EFFECTS OF MAINSTREAM EUROCENTRIC FEMINISM AND ANY MODERN CONSTRUCT OF HUMAN RELATIONS ESPECIALLY AS IT PERTAINS TO GENDER ROLES.

MOYA TELLS ME THAT SOCIETY HAS DECAYED BECAUSE WESTERN IDEOLOGIES HAVE BEEN ADOPTED BY THE EAST AND HAVE BECOME THE NORM. BUT WITH THE POWER OF YOU AND MOYA, I KNOW I CAN HELP THEM.

THANKS FOR LISTENING.

SINCERELY, YOU'RE INITIATE

''If They Can Lionize You They Can Sacrifice You'' - Thabang HA Mathapo

Dream Diary Entry

Dream Title:

____

What was the dream about?

____

____

____

____

____

Where it took place:

____

____

____

____

____

My interpretation:

____

____

____

Keywords/phrases spoken within the dream:

Dream symbols:

Note to Self:

Azanian Ti

By Phumzile Hadebe, March 30, 2008

One touch can cure anythi

Moses Kabinde is a 20-year-old University graduate who is able to heal people with his hands and mind. The Senegalese immigrant resides in New York and has a dedicated website where he sells merchandise, books, courses on self-improvement and healing consultations. Moses is preparing for a mass event which will take place in Los Angeles later this September in which he will heal over 700 people seated in a stadium and also conduct a one-on-one seminar for special guests who have paid the $23000 fee. It was at the age of 15, Adam says, that he began manifesting bizarre powers. "All these strange telekinetic things [started] happening around me. Just little things like pencils flying out of my hands, erasers flying out of my hands," he said. Moses says he wants to enter into impoverished public hospitals to heal diseases such as cancers and blood infections. Matilda Hendrix, an elderly nurse from Wisconsin, says she experienced the healing power of Moses' hands.

Azanian Ti

By Nomasonto Masela, April 1, 2008

3 Year old abandoned in ol

The last time Tobias was seen was when he was spotted running after a car with his German shepherd as it pulled away leaving him alone in a cemetery. He was taken in by a foster family while his family was trying to locate his whereabouts. News came out of a three-year-old boy who was abandoned with his pet dog in an Atlanta Georgia cemetery just two days before Christmas. A middle aged woman named Gwendolyn had reported the incident as the youngster tried to keep up with the fleeing car. This tragic event happened on a Wednesday at the Francis Memorial Gardens Cemetery in South Georgia. The witness said she called police when the boy and his dog were running after a red Chevrolet Tahoe. State patrol officers arrived and found the boy, who told them his name was Tobias and took the boy and his dog into protective custody. Because of negligence he was dumped at the cemetery. To many peoples surprise Tobias knew the first names of his mother and father but forgot where he lived.

R
fo
in

T
th
re
th
b
o
e
in
it
b
c
o

It
to
th
d

CHAPTER 5

THE CLONE

NOTE TO SELF: WHILE DEALING WITH CORPORATE CLIENTS

DEAR DIARY,

THE WORKPLACE IS FILLED WITH DIFFERENT PERSONALITIES AND AGENDAS. SOME PEOPLE WANT TO SABOTAGE OTHERS ON THEIR WAY TO THE TOP OF THE CORPORATE LADDER AND SOME WANT TO FOCUS ON WORK SO THEY CAN PROVIDE FOR THEIR FAMILIES. I AM WRITING A DETAILED MEMOIR ON A LETTER I JUST RECEIVED FROM A FRIEND WHO EXPERIENCED AN INCIDENT AT WORK LAST YEAR. MKHULU, PLEASE REMIND ME OF THIS INFORMATION SO THAT I CAN HAVE A FRAME OF REFERENCE FOR WHAT TO DO WHEN I ENCOUNTER SIMILAR ORDEALS FROM CLIENTS.

THIS NOTE IS ABOUT JOE TLADI, A 28-YEAR-OLD EMPLOYEE WORKING AT A BIG ACCOUNTING FIRM IN CAPE TOWN. JOE HAS EXPERIENCED A LOT LAST YEAR AND SAID HE CAME ACROSS THESE UNUSUAL CIRCUMSTANCES AFTER HIS PROMOTION TO A SENIOR LEVEL AT THE FIRM. JOE WAS PROMOTED TO A SENIOR SUPERVISORY POSITION AT THIS FIRM EARLY LAST YEAR AND WAS DOING WELL FOR THE FIRST 5 MONTHS.

WHEN JOE MOVED FROM WORKING ON THE SECOND FLOOR TO THE

8TH FLOOR, MOST OF THE COLLEAGUES WHO USED TO WORK WITH HIM ON THE SECOND FLOOR COULD NO LONGER SPEND LUNCHTIME WITH HIM. HE DEVELOPED NEW RELATIONSHIPS WITH OTHER COLLEAGUES IN THE BUILDING AND SOON STARTED SPENDING MOST OF HIS TIME WITH A NEW SOCIAL CIRCLE. DURING AN OFFICE BIRTHDAY OF ONE OF HIS FEMALE COLLEAGUES, HE STARTED NOTICING THAT HE WAS BEING WATCHED BY SOMEONE THE ENTIRE DAY.

THIS PERSON WAS LOOKING AT HIM AND STARING AT JOE AS OFTEN AS HE COULD REMEMBER THAT DAY. HE THEN APPROACHED THIS PERSON AND INTRODUCED HIMSELF SO HE COULD FIND OUT WHAT HE COULD HAVE POSSIBLY DONE WRONG. BUT THIS PERSON STRANGELY PRETENDED TO NOT EVEN NOTICE HIM OR UNDERSTAND WHERE HE WAS COMING FROM.

CURIOUS AS HE IS, JOE INVESTIGATED THIS PERSON'S BEHAVIOUR AND FOUND OUT THAT HIS NAME IS KGOMOTSO. KGOMOTSO HAS BEEN WORKING ON THE SECOND FLOOR WITH JOE FOR THE PAST 2 YEARS AND WAS PROMOTED WITH JOE AT THE SAME TIME IN DIFFERENT UNITS.

KGOMOTSO SEEMED TO BE A VERY WEIRD INDIVIDUAL BECAUSE HE HAD AN INSECURE DEMEANOUR ABOUT HIM THAT MADE JOE WORRIED.

WITH A STRANGE BEHAVIOUR KGOMOTSO HAD AN ECCENTRIC

CHARACTER AND WANTED PEOPLE (ESPECIALLY MEN) TO OBEY AND WORSHIP HIM LIKE A KING.

HE HAD WHAT MKHULU WOULD CALL THE MALE ATTENTION SEEKING AND VALIDATION THIRST ATTITUDE. BECAUSE JOE IS CONNECTED TO MOYA, HE ALWAYS PISSED OFF KGOMOTSO WHEN THEY WERE IN THE SAME ENVIRONMENT.

MANY PEOPLE AT THE COMPANY WERE SCARED OF HIM AND WERE EVEN FEARED BY TOP MANAGEMENT. JOE STARTED FEELING UNCOMFORTABLE BECAUSE EVERY TIME HE WOULD SAY ANYTHING KGOMOTSO WOULD COUNTER THE STATEMENT WITH AN OPPOSING OPINION. KGOMOTSO STARTED GROWING A GENERAL DISDAIN AND HATRED FOR JOE AFTER A WHILE BECAUSE JOE SEEMED TO BE SUCCEEDING IN LIFE.

JOE HAD BEEN SPIRITUALLY STRENGTHENED AT HIS CHURCH AND HAD BEEN RECEIVING BLESSINGS. WHETHER IT IS FINDING A NEW GIRLFRIEND WHO SUPPORTED HIM, BUYING A NEW CAR, AND FINALLY BEING ABLE TO ACCOMPLISH HIS PASSION AND DREAM FOR PLAYING THE PIANO, THINGS WERE LOOKING UP FOR HIM. THIS IRRITATED KGOMOTSO BECAUSE HE COULD FEEL THE SUCCESS OF JOE AND WANTED TO BECOME JOE.

A DEEP OBSESSION STARTED BUILDING IN KGOMOTSO'S HEART OVER TIME. WHEN JOE WENT TO SEE HIS BROTHER OVER A WEEKEND,

HE WAS TOLD BY MOYA THROUGH HIS BROTHER THAT HIS COLLEAGUE WAS OUT TO GET HIM. JOE WAS ALSO TOLD TO WATCH HIS BACK BECAUSE KGOMOTSO DOES NOT HAVE A PURE SOUL FROM THE CREATOR AS HE DOES.

HE WENT ON TO EXPLAIN THAT KGOMOTSO WAS A REINCARNATED DEMON PUT INTO A HUMAN HOST TO STEAL THE HOLY SPIRIT OF THE CHILDREN OF MOYA.

WHEN KGOMOTSO GETS HOME EVERY DAY HE GOES INTO HIS BEDROOM AND TAKES OF THE HUMAN FLESH THAT HE IS WEARING AND OPENS HIS CUPBOARD TO SPEAK TO HIS ANCESTRAL CREATOR WHO HAPPENS TO BE A DEAD WITCH.

THIS DEMONIC SPIRIT FEEDS ON THE UNIQUE SPIRIT OF GREAT PEOPLE WHICH COMES THROUGH THEIR AMAZING PURE HUMAN PERSONALITY AND GLOW.

KGOMOTSO IS A DESCENDENT OF A LONG LINE OF DEMONIC ENTITIES THAT USE THE MASK OF CORPSES TO WREAK HAVOC ON THE INNOCENT.

TRUTH OR MYTH

Masks of the Chokwe people are said to contain spirits that animate the alter ego of the person wearing it.

THEY DO SO BY MIMICKING THE BEHAVIOURS OF CERTAIN PEOPLE AND WHEN THEY'RE DONE THEY KIDNAP YOU SPIRITUALLY THROUGH A RITUAL THEY PERFORM ON THEMSELVES AND THEN THEY ATTACK YOU VIA WITCHCRAFT AT NIGHT AS THEY TRY TO KILL YOU.

IN JOE'S PREDICAMENT KGOMOTSO WAS TRYING TO ATTACK AND KILL HIM BUT COULD NOT SUCCEED. BECAUSE JOE IS A CHILD OF MOYA KGOMOTSO WAS UNABLE TO SHAPESHIFT AND STEAL HIS ESSENCE. THIS RESULTED IN KGOMOTSO DISAPPEARING AND HAS NEVER BEEN SEEN AGAIN. SOME PEOPLE GO TO WORK EVERY DAY TO STEAL OTHER PEOPLE'S ESSENCE, SPIRIT, OR GIFTS.

SOMETIMES THEY GO AS FAR AS TO TAKE PICTURES OF YOU AND PERFORM RITUALS AT HOME WITH THEIR DEMONIC ENTITIES OR FAMILY MEMBERS SO THAT THEY CAN BECOME YOU.

THIS NOTE I LEAVE FOR BOTH OF US SO WE CAN REFER BACK TO JOE'S STORY WHEN WE REQUIRE RESEARCH DEALING WITH WORKPLACE CASES.

WHEN WE USE OUR SACRED MOYA PRAYERS AGAINST THESE PEOPLE THEY START CHANGING BEHAVIOUR AROUND US BECAUSE THE POWER OF THE CREATOR CAN CUT THE SPELL AND LINK BETWEEN THEM AND THEIR DEMONIC CONSPIRERS.

NOT MANY OF THEM SUCCEED. SOME OF THEM VANISH OUT OF THIN

AIR WHILE OTHERS CAN REPRODUCE THEIR DEMONIC ESSENCE INTO THE WEAK HUMAN POPULATION. WHERE EVER THEY ARE THEY WILL NEVER SUCCEED.

I WILL HUNT THEM AND DEFEAT THEM WITH MOYA.

SINCERELY, YOU'RE INITIATE

"Unseen they come and unseen they go. Man in his ignorance calls them from below. Dark is the way the dark brothers travel, dark with a darkness not of the night, traveling over the earth they walk through man's dreams. Power have they gained from the darkness around them to call other dwellers from out of their plane, in ways that are dark and unseen by man. Into man's mind-space reach the dark brothers" - The Emerald Tablet of Tehuti

Dream Diary Entry

Dream Title:

____

What was the dream about?

____

____

____

____

____

Where it took place:

____

____

____

____

____

My interpretation:

____

____

____

Keywords/phrases spoken within the dream:

Dream symbols:

Note to Self:

Azanian Ti

By Duncan Mokhele, April 8, 2008

Oddly shaped Monolith dis

A strange oval shaped structure, around seven feet tall, became an instant hit among social media influencers after it was spotted at a park at Hatfield – Pretoria East last Thursday morning. After several posts of this mysterious object people began flocking to the park to take selfies in front of the structure. Citizen journalist say that this monolith is but one of many that have appeared and vanished in different parts of the world since December of 07. In Africa 12 sites have been located of these egg shaped, silver sorbets. The monolith appears to be an art piece in nature which some guess is made up of shiny steel sheets. Conspiracy theorists contemplate that this could be an extra-terrestrial space pod with a visitor from beyond the stars here to visit earthlings. They also ponder that NASA could also be behind it and could be using this object as a beacon of mind control through a hidden signal. The monolith has been a topic of much controversy as many influencers claim it is a campaign.

Azanian Ti

By Michael Viljoen, April 14, 2008

Extra-terrestrials left hum

Ancient Africans have encountered rare earth minerals in the past and have used these gems for spiritual purposes. From pharaohs to tribesmen, rare gems have always been sought after. To understand them from a contemporary African state of mind we have to ask ourselves, where are Rare Earth Elements Found? Geologists have made scientific breakthroughs in understanding the origins of rare earths. Most rare earth minerals are found deep beneath the earth's crust. Biological scientists also hypothesize that extra-terrestrial involvement could have been prevalent in earth having rare earth minerals. The primary economic sources of rare earths are the minerals bastnasite, monazite, and loparite and the lateritic ion-adsorption clays. When it comes to global natural resources, rare earths are primarily in four geologic environments: carbonatites, alkaline igneous systems, ion-adsorption clay deposits, and monazite-xenotime-bearing placer deposits.

CHAPTER 6

PINKY PINKY

DEAR MKHULU,

AS I WATCH THE NEWS, I KEEP SEEING THE VIOLENCE AND CONFLICT BETWEEN OUR PEOPLE WIDEN. MOSTLY BECAUSE OUR PEOPLE DO NOT UNDERSTAND HOW TO LOOK FOR ANSWERS TO CERTAIN PROBLEMS AND QUESTIONS. DAILY WE ARE CONFRONTED WITH NEWS ABOUT INFIDELITY, GREED, AND VIOLENCE. WE ARE NOW BEGINNING TO EXPERIENCE THE FIRST EMERGENCE OF GENDER-BASED VIOLENCE. THIS REMINDS ME OF A STORY I ONCE HEARD FROM A FRIEND WHILE WE WERE PLAYING MARBLES BACK IN PRIMARY SCHOOL.

MY FRIEND SPOKE OF HER COUSIN WHO AT THAT TIME RESIDED IN SOWETO WHEN HER LIFE CHANGED DRASTICALLY AT THAT MOMENT IN HER LIFE.

FOR THE SAKE OF KEEPING THIS PERSON'S IDENTITY A SECRET, WE WILL CALL HER JANE.

JANE GREW UP AS THE THIRD-BORN DAUGHTER TO A YOUNG COUPLE IN THE EAST AND AROUND THE TIME OF 1993. DUE TO ILLNESS HER FATHER PASSED AWAY AND WAS RAISED BY HER MOTHER IN SOWETO WHERE SHE ATTENDED HIGH SCHOOL. JANE EVENTUALLY COMPLETED HIGH SCHOOL AND WORKED AT A BIG RETAIL STORE IN

SANDTON FOR A WHILE AS SHE WAS NOT ABLE TO AFFORD MONEY FOR SCHOOLING.

WHILE WORKING AT THIS GROCERY STORE SHE MET 3 OTHER COLLEAGUES WITH WHO SHE DEVELOPED A RELATIONSHIP WITH AND THEY ALL BECAME SISTERS. THESE FOUR WOMEN WOULD HANG OUT WITH EACH OTHER AND BE EVEN CLOSE ENOUGH TO DISCUSS PERSONAL MATTERS AMONGST ONE ANOTHER. ON ONE WEEKEND JUST BEFORE THE EASTER HOLIDAYS, JANE RECEIVED A TEXT MESSAGE FROM HER FRIEND TELLING HER TO COME AND SEE HER AT A HOSPITAL.

WHEN JANE GOT TO THE HOSPITAL SHE FOUND OUT THAT HER FRIEND WAS RAPED BY THE STORES' MANAGER WHO GOES BY THE NAME, MARIUS.

MARIUS APPEARED TO BE A SUSPECTED WHITE SUPREMACIST AND HAD THE THIRD REICH TATTOO WITH THE NUMBER 14 ON HIS NECK.

BUT SECRETLY IT IS KNOWN THAT MALE WHITE SUPREMACISTS HAVE A FETISH FOR DARK-SKINNED BLACK WOMEN AND MOST WOULD EVEN SPY ON THEIR MAIDS WHEN THEY WERE GETTING DRESSED IN THEIR ROOMS.

MARIUS IS ALSO A SEX OFFENDER AND HAS BEEN RAPING MANY YOUNG GIRLS IN HIS NEIGHBOURHOOD.

THIS REVELATION CAME AS A SURPRISE TO JANE BECAUSE SHE COULDN'T UNDERSTAND HOW MARIUS WOULD RAPE HER FRIEND WHEN HE APPEARED TO EVERYONE AS BEING HAPPILY MARRIED. JANE LISTENED TO HER FRIEND WHILE SHE CRIED IN THE HOSPITAL BED. SHE WENT HOME IN THE AFTERNOON AND THOUGHT ABOUT WHAT HAPPENED TO HER FRIEND.

WHEN SHE ARRIVED AT WORK THE NEXT MORNING SHE WALKED PAST MARIUS'S OFFICE AND SAW THAT HE WAS LOOKING AT HER STRANGELY.

DURING A LUNCH BREAK, JANE WAS AT THE KITCHEN PREPARING FOOD FOR HERSELF, AND THEN MARIUS CAME AND CLOSED THE KITCHEN DOOR. HE TOLD HER THAT IF SHE WANTS TO KEEP HER JOB AND HER LIFE SHE WOULD KEEP QUIET AND NOT TELL A SOUL. FRIGHTENED BY THE THREATS SHE HAD BEEN TOLD, JANE FINISHED WORKING HER SHIFT AND TOOK A TAXI TO HER SISTER'HOUSE.

JANE'S OLDER SISTER WAS SPECIAL BECAUSE SHE HAD THE POWER OF SEEING AND CREATING SPIRITS WITH MOYA. WHEN JANE ENTERED THE HOUSE THAT MORNING SHE TOLD HER SHE WAS EXPECTING HER VISIT THAT DAY. THEY STARTED CHATTING AND EVENTUALLY HAD BREAKFAST IN THE LIVING ROOM WHEN JANE ANNOUNCED WHY SHE HAD VISITED HER. AFTER THEY DISCUSSED JANE'S COLLEAGUE SHE TOOK JANE TO A ROOM OUTSIDE THE HOUSE IN THE BACKYARD AND OPENED A METALLIC CHEST. INSIDE

THE CHEST WERE 3 PINK CANDLES, A SMALL PLASTIC BAG, AND A POWDERED WHITE SUBSTANCE NEXT TO A BIG AXE.

JANE ASKED WHAT THESE WERE AND SHE TOLD HER TO GRAB THE CONTENTS OF THE CHEST AND TAKE HER TO HER COLLEAGUE'S HOUSE. THEY RUSHED INTO THE CAR AND QUICKLY DROVE TO HER FRIEND'S HOUSE WHERE THEY FOUND HER IN THE BACKYARD WASHING CLOTHES AND DOING HER LAUNDRY. SHE BURST INTO TEARS AND HUGGED THEM BOTH AS THEY ENTERED THE RDP HOUSE.

ONCE IN, JANE'S SISTER EXPLAINS TO BOTH OF THEM WHAT SHE CAN DO TO HELP THEM. SHE DETAILS A RITUAL IN WHICH THEY WILL USE THE OBJECTS SHE HAS BROUGHT TO HER FROM OUT THE METALLIC CHEST AND SUMMON A SPIRIT CALLED PINKY-PINKY. PINKY-PINKY IS AN ANCIENT SPIRIT THAT WOULD BE ABLE TO HELP JANE'S COLLEAGUE AVENGE HERSELF AGAINST MARIUS.

JANE'S SISTER TOLD THE FRIEND THAT IF SHE WANTED REVENGE ON WHAT WAS DONE TO HER SHE CAN SUMMON PINKY-PINKY BY FOLLOWING THESE SIMPLE STEPS.

STEP 1: WALK INSIDE A PUBLIC FEMALE TOILET AND WAIT UNTIL EVERYONE IS OUT. LIGHT THE 3 CANDLES BESIDE THE MIRROR.

STEP 2: OPEN ALL THE TAPS OF ALL BASINS AND FLUSH ALL THE

TOILETS IN THE RESTROOM.

STEP 3: PUT THE AXE DOWN ON ONE OF THE DOORS IN THE ROOM IN ANY DIRECTION YOU WISH.

STEP 4: POUR THE WHITE POWDER ONTO YOUR LEFT-HAND PALM AND BLOW IT ON A MIRROR (ANY MIRROR).

THEN ONCE YOU ARE DONE SAY A PRAYER AND TELL PINKY-PINKY THAT YOU WANT VENGEANCE AND FOR HIM TO BRING BACK YOUR DIGNITY AS A WOMAN OF THE EARTH. ONCE YOU ARE DONE TAKE THE CANDLES, LEAVE THE AXE, AND WALK OUT. ONCE YOU HAVE COMPLETED THIS RITUAL CONTINUE WITH YOUR LIFE AND NEVER LOOK BACK AGAIN.

THEY BOTH LISTENED CAREFULLY AND AGREED THAT JANE'S FRIEND WOULD TAKE VENGEANCE AND FOLLOW THROUGH WITH THE RITUAL.

AS JANE AND HER SISTER LEFT, THE FRIEND LEFT WITH THEM AND WAS DROPPED OFF AT A PETROL STATION NEARBY WHERE THERE SEEMS TO BE A PUBLIC RESTROOM. JANE AND HER SISTER WENT HOME AS THEY LEFT THE FRIEND TO CONDUCT HER RITUAL.

THE NEXT MORNING WHEN JANE ARRIVED AT WORK EARLY IN THE MORNING EVERYONE AT WORK WAS GATHERED AROUND A COMPUTER

SCREEN AT THE ADMIN OFFICE WATCHING SURVEILLANCE FOOTAGE OF AN INCIDENT THAT HAPPENED THE PREVIOUS NIGHT WHEN THE STORE WAS CLOSED.

THE FOOTAGE WAS 5 MINUTES LONG AND SHOWED A TALL MAN WEARING A PINK SUIT, A WHITE FEDORA CAP WITH A CIGARETTE IN HIS MOUTH CREEPING BEHIND WHAT SEEMED TO LOOK LIKE MARIUS.

THE IDENTITY OF THE MYSTERIOUS MAN COULD NOT BE IDENTIFIED BUT HIS OUTFIT COULD. THE SURVEILLANCE TAPE SHOWS THE MAN STABBING MARIUS FROM THE BACK WITH A KNIFE AS HE RELIEVES HIMSELF ON A URINAL.

THE MYSTERIOUS MAN THEN BEATS HIM UP AND THEN URINATES ON HIS FACE BEFORE ENDING HIS LIFE BY STRIKING HIM ON THE HEAD WITH AN AXE.

THE POLICE WHO WERE LEADING THE INVESTIGATION AND DISPLAYING TO THEM WHAT HAD HAPPENED SAID THEY COULD NOT GATHER EVIDENCE BECAUSE THERE WERE NO FINGERPRINTS ON THE CRIME SCENE, THEY ALSO SAID THAT THE CAMERA'S AROUND THE BUILDING SHOW NO MAN ENTERING BESIDES MARIUS FOR THE PAST 2 HOURS BEFORE THE CRIME HAPPENED.

TRUTH OR MYTH

The Yoruba people of present-day Nigeria are the first to have an ax-wielding deity. Shango is the Orisha of thunder.

WHAT CONFUSES MANY PEOPLE ABOUT THE CASE EVEN TODAY IS THAT ONCE THE MAN MURDERS MARIUS HE PICKS UP HIS PHONE AND CALLS THE POLICE BUT IT'S A LITTLE GIRL'S VOICE THAT WAS HEARD AT THE POLICE STATION WHEN THE PHONE CALL WAS ANSWERED.

WAS THIS PINKY-PINKY?

WAS THIS REVENGE?

WAS THIS SOMEONE ELSE'S FATHER AVENGING THEIR DAUGHTERS' AGONY?

NO ONE KNOWS, MKHULU.

SINCERELY, YOU'RE INITIATE

"For we wrestle not against flesh and blood, but principalities, against powers, against the rulers of the darkness of this world, against spiritual wickedness in high places" - The Hebrew Bible

Dream Diary Entry

Dream Title:

____

What was the dream about?

____

____

____

____

____

Where it took place:

____

____

____

____

____

My interpretation:

____

____

____

Keywords/phrases spoken within the dream:

Dream symbols:

Note to Self:

Azanian Ti

By Brian Hamilton, April 18, 2008

Addicted to Video Games

It has been proven that 90% of video game players do not engage in video games in a harmful way or in a way that causes negative long term consequences. Only a small percentage of gamers become chronically addicted to video games and from this psychological strain they can suffer mentally, socially and behaviorally. Studies done by video game critics mark online gaming as an enjoyable form of entertainment. They have also conducted research and have concluded that spending too much time playing video games could also translate to negative developmental outcomes and can develop an addiction. Brandon Myers from the augmented reality assessment council in the UK has written a research paper detailing that 10% of gamers globally displayed higher levels of depression, aggression, shyness, problematic cell phone use and anxiety by evolving adulthood. Azanian Times confirms that there has not been a study linking video game addiction and drug abuse.

Azanian Ti

By Helen Qumisa, April 24, 2008

Big Foot spotted

There has been footage of a fury ape-like primate which circulated the web recently. Western urban legend theorists call this creature big foot a name given to a cave man looking being. This short video clip is taken near the Caucus Mountains of Europe the figure bears a likeness to a humanoid or ape with limbs and hands. A longer version was uploaded on online forums. This mysterious animal appears to be covered in grey and black fur, which matches the description of the mythical creature which has been written about in Nordic mythological folklore. A group of Russian fisherman have also made claims of seeing unusual beast-like figures in the rocky slopes of Siberia. The men describe the being as a 7 foot giant with big hands and feet. They told a local newspaper that the being had a rock in one hand and a fish in another. Apparently this primate also has a family because it was seen escaping with a small infant on its back. A middle aged Gypsy woman from Georgia a couple of miles east from the Caucus.

CHAPTER 7

A MEMOIR ON THE BROTHERS AND SISTERS OF DARKNESS

DEAR MKHULU,

MOYA GAVE ME A VISION INTO A FORGOTTEN PAST AND MISUNDERSTOOD PRESENT. WHAT I SAW WAS AMAZING AND SCARY AT THE SAME TIME. HISTORY, AS WE KNOW IT TODAY, IS NOTHING BUT A LIE THAT NEEDS TO BE CORRECTED. WE ARE TOLD BY FORGOTTEN SCRIPTURES ABOUT ANCIENT SUPERIOR BEINGS THAT WALKED THE EARTH ALONGSIDE OUR ANCESTORS BUT ARE NOT TOLD WHERE THESE BEINGS ORIGINATED FROM.

THE ANCIENT SCRIPTURES DETAIL A HISTORY OF THE FORMING OF THE EARTH AND ENTITIES WHICH EXISTED AT THE BEGINNING OF MANKIND AND THE GALAXY. WHAT HAS BEEN COUNTLESSLY LEFT OUT IS THE ORIGINS OF THOSE BEINGS BEFORE THEIR INVOLVEMENT WITH OUR REALITY. MOYA SHOWS ME THE CREATION OF WHAT SEEMS TO LOOK LIKE A RED PLANET WITH A RING AROUND ITS SUN.

THESE BEINGS ARE CREATED AND GIVEN DOMINION OVER THIS PLANET TO RULE AND LIVE IN HARMONY.

THE BEINGS ARE GIANTS AND ARE VERY DIFFERENT IN APPEARANCE AND RANK. THERE IS A WARRIOR CLASS, AN INTELLECTUAL CLASS,

AND A SPIRITUAL CLASS OF THE BEINGS OF THIS WORLD.

THERE ARE LEADERS AND FOLLOWERS WITH ADVANCED SOCIETIES AND CORRUPTED CIVILIZATIONS SPREADING ACROSS THIS WORLD AS TIME GOES BY.

THESE BEINGS CAN HARVEST AND ABSORB ENERGY FROM THEIR SUN, BY OPENING AN EYE THAT SEEMS TO BE ON THEIR FOREHEADS. THIS RINGED SUN THEY GET ENERGY FROM SEEMS TO HAVE AN OBJECT WHICH LOOKS LIKE A CUBE ON TOP OF IT. THIS OBJECT IS IN A CONSTANT STATE OF MOVEMENT AND SHIFTS ANTI-CLOCKWISE.

THEY SPEAK AND COMMUNICATE BY FLASHING IMAGES AT EACH OTHER.

THESE IMAGES LOOK LIKE SYMBOLS AND CAN BE IMPRINTED INTO A MIND TO BE USED WHEN NEEDED.

THERE IS NO PLANT LIFE OR ANY OTHER LIVING ORGANISM ON THIS PLANET AND OXYGEN IS A THICK MISTY SUBSTANCE THAT SMELLS LIKE PETROLEUM GAS. I AM BEING SHOWN A BRIGHT LIGHT AS IT MAKES ITS WAY TO THE PLANET BY A MYSTERIOUS ENTITY ABOVE.

AS TIME GOES BY THE RING SUN STARTS TO WEAKEN AND IS NOW STARTING TO LOSE ITS ENERGY AND GLOW.

IN A FRANTIC HASSLE, THE STRANGE BEINGS START TO CHANGE

THEIR BEHAVIOUR. THEY BEGIN TO CHANGE FORM AND START TO SHED THEIR GLOWING METALLIC SURFACES.

THE BEINGS ARE THEN SHOWN TO ME AS BRIGHT HUMANOID VESSELS AS THEY START TO MAKE SOUNDS WITH THEIR WINGS. THEY CAN KILL AND IMPALE EACH OTHER.

BY MURDERING ONE ANOTHER THE ONES THAT ARE LEFT WILL BE ABLE TO HAVE MORE ENERGY FOR THEMSELVES.

IT CAME TO PASS THAT THE RED PLANET'S SUN LOST ITS RINGS AND WAS REMOVED OUT OF ITS ORBIT BY A MORE POWERFUL AND RADIANT SUN.

THIS CAUSED THE BEINGS TO SEEK REFUGE AMONGST THE STARS OF THE GALAXY AS THEIR HOME WAS GOING TO BE DESTROYED. THE ANCESTORS ALSO TEACH US THAT THE CREATOR DECIDED TO END THE PREVIOUS UNIVERSE AND BEGIN A NEW ONE BECAUSE THE ONE HE CREATED, IN THE BEGINNING, LACKED BEINGS WITH SOULS.

THEN WHEN MY VISION FADED I WAS ALSO SHOWN THE CREATION OF OUR UNIVERSE. ONCE THE RED PLANET WAS DESTROYED AND ITS SUN DRAINED OF ENERGY, THE WHOLE UNIVERSE WAS SHUTDOWN. ALL THERE WAS, WERE DARKNESS AND AN INFINITE VOID OF NOTHINGNESS. BUT BECAUSE OF THE CREATORS' WILL THE NEW

SUN WAS REVEALED AND LIGHT BEGAN AGAIN.

MOYA SHOWS ME THAT OUT OF THIS WATER OF BLAZING LIGHT AND HEAT CAME NEW STARS AND WORLDS ARE BEING CREATED. THE BEINGS FROM THE PREVIOUS DIMENSION EMERGE FROM THE STARS AND WATCH AS A NEW UNIVERSE WAS CREATING HERSELF. FINALLY, THE EARTH CAME INTO BEING AND GAVE BIRTH TO THE ANCESTORS OF MOYA, THE CHILDREN OF LIGHT.

THE RED PLANET BEINGS SAW US AND BECAME JEALOUS OF OUR GRANDEUR. WE ARE CREATED IN BALANCE THROUGH THE CREATOR AND WITHIN THE UNIVERSE. SEEING OUR GREAT FUTURE, THE RED PLANET CITIZENS PLOTTED TO INTERVENE IN OUR HUMAN STORY.

HALF OF THEM FELL FROM THE STARS AND USED THEIR EYE TO FUSE WITH OUR MOTHERS. THEY IMPREGNATED THEM AND BORE THE BROTHERS AND SISTERS OF DARKNESS.

WE SAW THIS HAPPEN OVER TIME AS THE OFFSPRING THEY SPAWNED LACKED COMPASSION AND WAS NOT SPIRITUALLY BALANCED WITH THE CREATORS' SPIRIT.

USING THE POWER OF MOYA OUR FATHERS BEGAN TO RETALIATE. SOME SURVIVED AND SOME EVENTUALLY DIED. WE TOOK REFUGE WITHIN THE EARTH TO HIDE FROM THESE BROTHERS AND SISTERS BUT STRUGGLED FOR MANY CENTURIES AGAINST THEM.

TRUTH OR MYTH

The ancient Egyptian crook and flail are symbols conveying the subjugation of the human lower self. The human ego was considered demonic.

WHEN THE OTHER HALF OF THE RED PLANET BEINGS SAW OUR STRUGGLE THEY PITIED US AND WANTED TO HELP US. THESE BECAME OUR DEITIES, GUARDIANS, AND GODS WHO FOUGHT SIDE BY SIDE WITH US AGAINST THE DARKNESS.

WE BUILT GIANT TEMPLES AND MEGALITHIC STRUCTURES IN THEIR NAME SO THAT WE COULD GIVE THEM A PIECE OF OUR ENERGY FOR STRENGTH IN BATTLE. THEY FOUGHT ALONGSIDE US FOR MANY MILLIONS OF YEARS UNTIL THE DARKNESS CAME UP WITH A PLAN. THE BROTHERS AND SISTERS OF DARKNESS SAW THAT THEY COULD DISAPPEAR AND BECOME INVISIBLE BY HIDING IN THE SPIRIT REALM BUT THEY ALSO DISCOVERED THAT THEY COULD ALSO DESTROY USING DARK MAGIC.

THE WAR STOPPED FROM BEING A PHYSICAL WAR TO BEING A SPIRITUAL WAR. NOT BEING ABLE TO SEE THE ENEMY, OUR DEITIES TRANSPORTED THEMSELVES INTO THE SPIRITUAL REALM AND BECAME WHAT WE TODAY CALL THE FOUR ELEMENTS. THESE ARE THE ELEMENTS THAT WE USE TO FIGHT AGAINST THE DARKNESS. THE FIFTH ELEMENT IS WITHIN US AND IS THE POWER OF MOYA.

THE CREATIVE POWER OF THE CREATOR IS PASSED DOWN TO US FROM OUR ANCESTORS AND PROTECTED BY OUR DEITIES. TODAY WE BATTLE THEIR DESCENDANTS AND WITH THE HELP OF MOYA – WE ARE WINNING. THERE WILL ALWAYS BE CASUALTIES IN WARFARE BUT OUR FAMILY WILL NOT DIE IN VAIN AGAINST THIS EVIL.

NO MATTER WHAT POSITIONS OF POWER THEY MIGHT BE CONSOLIDATING WE WILL NEVER GO GENTLY INTO ANY GOOD NIGHT.

THE FIGHT CONTINUES...

PREPARE YOURSELF MKHULU.

SINCERELY, YOU'RE INITIATE

"Whatever has happened, has happened for good. Whatever is happiness is also for good. Whatever will happen, shall also be good.

What have you lost that you cry for?
What did you bring, that you have lost?
What did you create that was destroyed?
What you have taken, has been from here
What you gave has been given here
What belongs to you today, belonged to someone yesterday and will be someone else's tomorrow
Change is the law of the universe"

- The Bhagavadgita

Dream Diary Entry

Dream Title:

What was the dream about?

Where it took place:

My interpretation:

Keywords/phrases spoken within the dream:

Dream symbols:

Note to Self:

Azanian T

By Timothy Michaels, April 26, 2008

Man Wins Lottery twice

Bongani, a 67 year old truck driver from Simonsville, Cape Town, won a R800, 000 prize from a scratch-off ticket he bought last summer. Bongani or Bongz (for short) had already won a jackpot of R2 million from another lottery draw ticket in March. Some would think that winning R2 million in a space of six months would lead a person to irresponsible spending, but Bongz tells Azanian Times that not much has changed for him despite his bank balance. Bongz continues to work at a local fried chicken franchise, where he delivers meals to the residents throughout the day. Bongz also tells our reporter that he waited a week to hand in his winning ticket — not because he wanted time to process the win, but because that was the earliest his work timetable would allow, to give him enough time off to drive 1 hour to the Lottery headquarters in Simonsville. After a consultation with his financial adviser Bongz began working on his house. Instead of buying a mansion.

Azanian Ti

By Jim Ngobeni, April 28, 2008

Alien abduction gone wron

In the town of Emalahleni in Mpumalanga a secret society of approximately 1500 members gather every Saturday for a meeting. Two Sisters Jane and Barbara (both wish to remain anonymous), who have been attending these meetings, have driven 25 km to come and share their experiences with regard to the alien conspiracies plaguing the community. This group which was previously a support group for gambling, alcohol, drugs and sex addition, now goes by the name Ngwedi. This group specializes to those who say they've been in contact of have been abducted by aliens. Humans have wondered if they were the only beings in the universe or if they are sharing this universe with other life forms unknown. In a 2000 people poll survey that was done by the scientific community, nearly half of all Africans and millions more globally believe were not alone. Close to 50 million Africans on the continent claim they have seen or know someone who has seen a UFO. While a growing younger population believe they have met aliens.

CHAPTER 8

LORD OF A MAGIC RING

DEAR MKHULU,

I WAS AT THE LOCAL GROCERY STORE OVER THE WEEKEND AND WHILE SHOPPING, I SAW A TALL DARK-SKINNED BLACK MAN AT THE MEAT AISLE WITH A STRANGE OBJECT ON HIS FINGER. HE SEEMED TO BE FROM WEST AFRICA AS I COULD HEAR HIS ACCENT AND LANGUAGE DIALECT WHEN SPEAKING TO OTHERS. THIS MAN HAD A MAGIC RING ON HIS FINGER AND MADE ME DIZZY WHEN I WAS NEAR IT. I COULD HEAR VOICES IN MY HEAD OF ANCESTORS SPEAKING TO ME.

SOME TELLING ME TO GO BACK TO THE CAR BECAUSE THE ENERGY OF THE RING COULD GIVE ME A HEADACHE AS I AM A SON OF MOYA. I QUICKLY LEFT MY GROCERY BASKET AND RUSHED TO THE PARKING LOT RIGHT INTO THE CAR SO I COULD BREATHE AND RELAX FOR A FEW MINUTES. ONCE IN THE CAR A STRANGE SPIRIT ENTERED THE BACK SEAT AND INTRODUCED ITSELF AS THE RING MAKER.

HE SAID HE APOLOGIZED FOR THE DISTURBANCE HE CAUSED ME AND WANTED TO PROPOSE SOMETHING TO ME AND YOU SEEING THAT WE POSSESSED THE SAME VIBRATORY FIELD.

THE RING MAKER TOLD ME THAT HE IS 2000 YEARS OLD AND WAS

BORN IN A SMALL VILLAGE NEXT TO THE NIGER RIVER. BEFORE HE COULD TELL ME SPECIFICALLY WHAT HE WANTED FROM ME HE SPOKE OF A LEGEND.

THIS LEGEND INVOLVES THE FOUR CORNERS OF THE AFRICAN CONTINENT AND THE BEGINNING OF THE AFRICAN TRIBES WHICH LATER BECAME THE MANY CULTURES THAT WE HAVE TODAY.

HE TOLD ME THAT WHAT I SAW IN THE STORE WAS A MAGIC JINN RING CREATED FOR MEDIEVAL WEST AFRICAN KINGDOMS BY HIM HUNDREDS OF YEARS AGO FOR A SPIRITUAL PURPOSE.

HE FURTHER EXPOUNDED TO ME OF AN AGE THOUSANDS OF YEARS AGO ACROSS THE CONTINENT, WHEN THE ATMOSPHERE CHANGED AND CAUSED A BIOLOGICAL DECAY WITHIN THE MELANATED DNA OF OUR PEOPLE.

HE SPOKE OF A TIME WHEN WE WERE TALL AND STRONGER THAN TODAY AND HAD SUPERIOR PSYCHO-SPIRITUAL INTELLIGENCE WHICH ALLOWED THE STRONGEST AMONGST US TO HARNESS THE POWER OF THE COSMOS TO MANIPULATE THE ELEMENTAL WORLD.

HE SAID THAT WHEN THIS ENVIRONMENTAL CHANGE BROKE US DOWN WE LOST OUR CONNECTION TO OUR SURROUNDINGS AND EACH OTHER. THE KINGS AND MYSTICS OF THAT TIME RELIED ON ELEMENTAL SPIRITS TO HELP THEM RUN THEIR SOCIETIES AND CIVILIZATIONS.

THE RING MAKER SAID THE CHANGING ECOLOGY WEAKENED THE CONTROL THAT THE ELITES HAD IN THOSE SOCIETIES. A GROUP OF BLACKSMITHS FROM ALL OVER THE CONTINENT CAME TOGETHER ONE DAY IN A TEMPLE AND HAD A CONFERENCE DETAILING A STRATEGY OF WHAT TO MAKE OF THIS NEW PHENOMENON. AFTER HOURS OF DISCUSSIONS AND DEBATES, THEY DECIDED TO PULL OUT THEIR ANCIENT TALISMAN-MAKING SPELLBOOK.

THIS SPELL BOOK HAD INSTRUCTIONS ON HOW TO MAKE ENERGY TALISMANS AND RINGS TO BRING FORTH A CERTAIN CHANGE IN THE ELECTROMAGNETIC FIELD OF THE EARTH THROUGH ONE'S WILL AND INTENTION.

THE RING MAKER THEN SHOWED ME A VISION OF THE RINGS THAT WERE DESIGNED BY THE SORCERERS OF AFRICA AND THEN I SAW MANY WITH EXOTIC SHAPES AND CRYSTALS PLACED WITHIN THEM. HE FURTHER TOLD ME OF THE DIFFERENT MAGIC RINGS THAT CAN BE MADE FOR DIFFERENT INTENTIONS.

HE SAID SOME OF THE MAGIC RINGS HE MADE WERE FOR THE FOLLOWING:

POLITICAL RING: THIS RING IS MADE WITH A LION'S PAW AND IS INTENDED TO HELP THE WEARER WITH POLITICAL BATTLES AND TO HYPNOTIZE LARGE CROWDS OF PEOPLE SO THAT ELECTIONS CAN BE WON.

LOVE RINGS: THIS RING IS MADE WITH A RED ROSE AND IS INTENDED TO MAKE SOMEONE FALL IN LOVE WITH YOU.

THIS RING MAGNIFIES YOUR SEX APPEAL AND MAKES THE OPPOSITE SEX WANT YOU SEXUALLY.

MONEY RINGS: A MONEY RING IS MADE FROM SNAKE VENOM AND CAN HELP ATTRACT MONEY TO YOUR LIFE. THIS CAN ALSO HELP EXPAND YOUR EMPIRE AND MAKE YOUR BUSINESS UNSTOPPABLE.

WAR RING: THIS IS THE MOST DANGEROUS RING OF ALL. THE AGGRESSIVE WAR RING MAKES YOU DOMINATE WARS AND CHEAT DEATH. BUT IT COMES WITH A PRICE. YOU HAVE TO GIVE YOUR SOUL AWAY IN EXCHANGE FOR THE POWER OF THE RING AND CAN ONLY HAVE YOUR SOUL BACK ONCE YOU TAKE OFF THE RING. IF YOU DIE IN POSSESSION OF THIS RING YOUR SPIRIT COULD STAY ON EARTH AND NOT BE ABLE TO COMPLETELY ENTER THE ANCESTRAL PLANE.

TRUTH OR MYTH

Metaphysicians propose that animism and idolatry are two different things.

THERE ARE MANY MORE RINGS THAT WERE CREATED BY THESE WISE MEN. THESE RINGS WERE TOO POWERFUL TO BE IN THE SAME REGION. THE RINGS HAD TO BE SPREAD ACROSS THE CONTINENT AND SHARED AMONGST THE ARISTOCRATS OF EVERY NATION. ANYONE WITH THE RECIPE CAN REPRODUCE THE RING. EVERY TRIBE HAS BLOODLINES AND CAN MANUFACTURE SPECIFIC RINGS BASED ON THEIR ANCESTRY.

THE RING MAKER TOLD ME, THIS IS THE REASON WHY THERE ARE SO MANY TRIBES AND THE RING IS WHAT COULD HAVE CAUSED THEM TO SEPARATE EVEN MORE.

THERE WERE COUNTLESS WARS OVER THESE RINGS AND SOME OF THEM WERE FOR POWER AND CONTROL. THE RING MAKER SAID ONLY A PERSON GIFTED WITH MOYA CAN BE ABLE TO CREATE THESE RINGS. HE TOLD ME THAT HE PROPOSES THAT I START MAKING MAGIC RINGS WITH HIS GUIDANCE AND ASSISTANCE. HE SAID THAT I SHOULD TELL YOU IF YOU COULD ALSO ALLOW ME TO MAKE NEW RINGS FOR HEALTH AND EMPLOYMENT PURPOSES FOR CLIENTS. I KNOW THAT YOU ARE EXTREMELY KNOWLEDGEABLE ABOUT SPIRITUALITY AND ENERGY.

AFTER SPEAKING WITH HIM HE SAID HE WILL GIVE ME A WEEK TO THINK ABOUT THIS AND DISCUSS IT WITH YOU FIRST BEFORE A DECISION IS MADE. I FOR ONE DO NOT THINK WE HAVE TO, AS THERE ARE ALREADY PEOPLE DOING IT AND WE BOTH DO NOT SPECIALIZE

IN PHYSICAL MAGICAL OBJECTS.

I LEAVE THIS REVELATION TO YOU. IF YOU FEEL LIKE WE SHOULD CREATE RINGS THEN I WILL GLADLY GATHER THE NECESSARY TOOLS AND MAKE CONTACT WITH THE RING MAKER, TO BEGIN WITH, LESSONS. IF YOU REFUSE THEN THAT IS OKAY WITH ME.

I JUST WANTED TO INFORM YOU OF WHAT TOOK PLACE OVER THE WEEKEND.

SINCERELY, YOU'RE INITIATE

"It is no measure of health to be well adjusted to a profoundly sick society" - Jiddu Krishnamurti

Dream Diary Entry

Dream Title:

___

What was the dream about?

___

___

___

___

___

Where it took place:

___

___

___

___

___

My interpretation:

___

___

___

Keywords/phrases spoken within the dream:

Dream symbols:

Note to Self:

Azanian Ti

By Thami Sambhuza, April 30, 2008

Animals can speak

Scientific research from the international institute of animal communication has proved that killer whales have the ability to mimic the complex phonetics of human speech. Olga Samuels, the author of the ground breaking textbook "creatures of sound" has headed this study. Professor Aldridge Lamar from the African American research academy of animal sciences has led a team of professionals in late 2006 to Asia and proved that Orangutans are able to move their vocal cords in a way that is almost similar to humans. This study was conducted on an Ape from Cambodia, who after a month of practices by a trained veterinarian could utter two words. In July of 2006 at the Elephant Centaury in Varanasi India, an American tourist captured footage of a male elephant communicating using gestures in a human way. This elephant was able to create sounds by placing its trunk into its mouth and moving his head from left to right. This discovery is no way new to but has been hidden from mainstream society for years.

Azanian Ti

By Mandisa Qunta, June 10, 2008

Time traveler hints at alien

An abnormally tall man found mysteriously off the shore of a Mozambican beach early this year claims he is a time traveler on a mission to warn the human species of an alien invasion taking place by year 2021 on earth. According to numerous reports, this man has been arrested on charges of public indecency and disturbance because he was walking naked in the city while telling people his story. This man who has been identified as Issa Mansu, a man who controversially went missing 80 years ago in Uganda. He has managed to retain his youth because he says he has been sleeping beneath the ocean in a time capsule created by aliens in the middle of what is called the Bermuda triangle. Our Mozambican correspondent says the man did not want to speak to any government official but only to the common individual. He told a local farmer that he was able to time travel because the aliens had genetically altered his body using a black substance turning him into a biological space suit.

CHAPTER 9

THE HEART IS THE DRUM

DEAR MKHULU,

TODAY AFRICANS ARE BLESSED WITH THE GIFT OF CREATIVITY FROM ALL WALKS OF LIFE. SINGING AND DANCING PLAY A BIG ROLE IN AFRICAN CULTURE AND NOT MANY PEOPLE KNOW WHY THIS IS SO. SOUTHERN AFRICA IS HOME TO THE DRUM AND THE PIANO BUT THE DESCENDANTS THEMSELVES DO NOT KNOW THEIR HISTORY. THERE WAS A POINT IN TIME WHEN THERE WAS NO MUSIC IN THE WORLD. PEOPLE LIVED THEIR LIVES IN SILENCE AND HAD NO DEEP CONNECTION WITH EACH OTHER.

MOST MARRIAGES AND RELATIONSHIPS WERE ARRANGED AND PLANNED BY ELDERS SO THAT BLOODLINES COULD BE CONTROLLED AMONGST CERTAIN FAMILIES FOR FINANCIAL PURPOSES.

THIS CAUSED AN ISSUE FOR THE OFFSPRING OF TWO FAMILIES WHO RESIDED IN A MOUNTAIN VILLAGE IN NORTHERN MAPUNGUBWE. THESE WERE TWO MIDDLE-CLASS FAMILIES OF THE DUMBA AND THE DJEMBE CLAN.

THESE FAMILIES LIVED ON OPPOSITE ENDS OF THE SAME HILL OF THABA SKUBU AND HAD NEVER SPOKEN TO EACH OTHER BEFORE.

THERE WAS A DISAGREEMENT BETWEEN BOTH OF THEIR ANCESTORS HUNDREDS OF YEARS AGO BEFORE THE BANTU MIGRATION.

SINCE THIS CONFLICT BETWEEN THE FAMILIES, BOTH FAMILIES HAVE SWORN TO NEVER BE WITH EACH OTHER BUT OUT OF PRIDE, THEY BOTH DECIDED TO LIVE NEXT TO EACH OTHER.

THESE TWO FAMILIES HATED EACH OTHER WITH A PASSION. EVERYONE ACROSS THE NORTH KNEW ABOUT THIS. THEY WOULD WALK IN SEPARATE PATHS WHEN IN THE SAME ENVIRONMENT OR WOULD NOT EVEN LET THEIR CATTLE GRAZE NEAR EACH OTHER'S PASTURES.

OUT OF THIS DEEP DISLIKE BETWEEN THESE TWO SIMILAR FAMILIES, THEY BOTH DECIDED TO BUILD A WALL BETWEEN THEIR ESTATES SO THEY WOULD NEVER BE ABLE TO BE IN PHYSICAL SIGHT OF ONE ANOTHER AGAIN.

THESE TWO FAMILIES EACH HAD A DAUGHTER AND SON OF WHICH ONE WAS A BOY AND THE OTHER A GIRL OF A SIMILAR AGE GROUP. THE DUMBA FAMILY'S SON GREW UP TO BE AN ACCOMPLISHED TRADER AND WAS ONE OF THE MOST EDUCATED BUSINESSMEN IN THE NORTH, HE WAS EVEN FRIENDS WITH THE ROYAL TREASURER AND HAD CONNECTIONS THAT STRETCHED OVERSEAS.

THE DJEMBE FAMILY'S DAUGHTER GREW UP TO BECOME ONE OF

THE MOST BEAUTIFUL WOMEN IN THE WORLD AND WAS A VERY EDUCATED AND RESPECTED MEDICAL DOCTOR.

SHE SPECIALIZED IN NEUROSCIENCES AND RAN AN AFRICAN NEUROSCIENCE ACADEMY FOR THE YOUNG PEOPLE OF THE NORTH.

BOTH WERE WELL KNOWN AND HAD RELATIONSHIPS IN THE HIGHEST ROYAL DYNASTIES IN ALL THE ASIATIC NATIONS OF THE TIME. AS THE TIME CAME TO PASS THEIR PATHS CROSSED AND THESE TWO YOUNG ADULTS BOTH MET EACH OTHER. NOT KNOWING ONE ANOTHER'S FAMILY BACKGROUND OR CLAN NAMES THEY SPOKE AND WOULD GO ON DATES TOGETHER BY THE NORTHERN RIVER AT A PRESTIGIOUS RESTAURANT FOR OVER A YEAR.

THIS BECAME AN ISSUE AS ONE NIGHT THEY SAW EACH OTHER'S FAMILY COAT OF ARMS AT A BANQUET OF WHICH THEY ATTENDED SEPARATELY AS AN INVITE TO THEIR FAMILIES. THEY BOTH WERE FRIGHTENED AND SWORE NOT TO TELL ANYONE. FOR THE FIRST TIME IN A WHILE, THEY WENT WEEKS NOT BEING ABLE TO SEE EACH OTHER. AFTER A WHILE, THEY DECIDED TO MEET BY THE GREAT SHONA WALL. AT THE END OF THAT DAY, THEY KISSED AND WERE SEEN BY A FAMILY FRIEND OF BOTH THE TWO FAMILIES WHO WAS A SPY FOR THE NATIONS' CHIEF.

THEY WENT BACK HOME AND PRETENDED AS NOTHING HAPPENED. BOTH OF THEIR FAMILIES HEARD ABOUT THEIR SECRET LOVE AFFAIR

AND ASSIGNED 24-HOUR BODYGUARDS TO EACH OF THEM TO MAKE SURE THEY COULDN'T SEE EACH OTHER AGAIN. THIS BECAME DREADFUL TO THE LOVERS AND MADE THEM QUESTION THEIR RELATIONSHIP.

OPTIMISTIC AS HE WAS THE DUMBA SON DECIDED TO BUY A MESSENGER EAGLE TO SEND HIS GIRLFRIEND LOVE LETTERS BUT THE EAGLE WAS STRUCK DOWN BY A SECURITY GUARD AT THE DJEMBE ESTATE ON-SITE, WITH A BOW AND ARROW. THEN THE DJEMBE DAUGHTER SENT A WILD RABBIT TO THE DUMBA PALACE BUT THE RABBIT WAS LATER INFECTED WITH AN UNKNOWN ENVIRONMENTAL DISEASE AND DIED IN THE FOREST ONE AFTERNOON.

THEY TRIED EVERYTHING AND COULD NOT MANAGE TO EFFECTIVELY COME UP WITH A STRATEGY FOR THEM TO BE ABLE TO COMMUNICATE WITHOUT BEING CAUGHT.

IN A SAD ATTEMPT TO CONNECT, THEY BOTH DECIDED TO PRAY TO THE MOON GODDESS FOR DIRECTION ON WHAT TO DO.

THE NEXT DAY A SPIRIT APPEARED TO BOTH OF THEM BY THE NAME OF LERATO AND GAVE THEM INSTRUCTIONS ON BUILDING AN OBJECT THAT THEY CAN BOTH USE TO COMMUNICATE WITH EACH OTHER'S SPIRIT THROUGH THE HEART CHAKRA.

TRUTH OR MYTH

Ancient Africans believed the heart contains brain cells as well.

THE SPIRIT TOLD THEM TO EACH BUILD IT USING A CLAY POT AND A PIECE OF COW SKIN TIGHTLY COVERED ON TOP SO THAT WHEN THEY STRUCK THE TOP OF THIS OBJECT A SOUND WOULD EMIT A FREQUENCY WAVE.

SHE TOLD THEM THAT AS LONG AS THEY WERE BOTH IMPRISONED BY SOCIETY THEY WOULD BE ABLE TO EMIT THE SOUND WITHOUT ANYONE ELSE HEARING IT AND BE ABLE TO COMMUNICATE WITHOUT INTERFERENCE.

THIS TO THEM WAS A BLESSING AND THEY BOTH CRAFTED THESE OBJECTS AND USED THEM FOR THE NEXT 4 MONTHS WITHOUT BEING CAUGHT.

THESE OBJECTS THEN BEGAN TO CHANGE SHAPE AND THE SOUND BECAME DEEPER WITH A POWERFUL BASE AS THEY BOTH MATURED INTO LOVE. SOMETIMES AT NIGHT THEY COULD SYNCHRONIZE THEIR HEARTS WITH THE VIBRATION OF THE OBJECT AND SEND EACH OTHER SENSUALLY SEDUCTIVE SOUNDS.

THIS OBJECT IS CALLED THE DRUM TODAY AND ITS SOUND CAN BE HEARD WHEN PLAYED BY ANYONE.

THE INSTRUMENT WAS BIRTHED OUT OF LOVE AND FROM THE SOUND OF THE HEARTBEAT WHEN JOY IS FELT.

SOME SAY WE CAN HEAR THE DRUM BECAUSE THE COUPLE EVENTUALLY RAN AWAY FROM HOME SO THEY COULD BE TOGETHER AND SOME SAY WE CAN HEAR THE DRUM BECAUSE THEIR LOVE FOR EACH OTHER WAS TOO POWERFUL TO BE FORGOTTEN.

AFRICA IS FILLED WITH BEAUTY.

SINCERELY, YOU'RE INITIATE

''How we live is different from how we ought to live that he who studies what ought to be done rather than what is done will learn the way to his downfall rather than his preservation''- Niccolò Machiavelli

Dream Diary Entry

Dream Title:

____

What was the dream about?

____

____

____

____

____

Where it took place:

____

____

____

____

____

My interpretation:

____

____

____

Keywords/phrases spoken within the dream:

Dream symbols:

Note to Self:

Azanian Ti

By Chris Modawu, June 14, 2008

Asteroid from another gala

Venus 777, an asteroid which has been orbiting the earth has been located by a group of graduate scientists in Tunisia. This has sparked controversy because this asteroid has been moving in a triangular prism shape. Fatima Muhammad from the Cairo museum has taken to social media and has shared images of hieroglyphs depicting an object circling the earth. She has also posted images of the ancient Egyptians building pyramids on other planets using the asteroid rock. The Tunisian scholars who made this discovery have said they are currently building a satellite that will be able to trace this asteroid and countless others from the middle of the Sahara. Most asteroids that live within the earth's orbit are known to be difficult to find because of their close proximity to the sun. This satellite (named "baby Horus" in Arabic) will therefore be able to track and study such objects during brief periods of time. According to their research many asteroids orbit planets whenever there is a planetary alignment.

Azanian Ti

By Francis Van Der Westhuizen, June 16, 2008

Kings of the jungle escape

Two lions and two tigers escaped from their enclosures in a German zoo for a whole day but were later reportedly back in their cages. The local residents near and living around the zoo were advised to stay indoors while the predators were on the loose. Later on a jaguar also escaped following the two lions and tigers out of its enclosure at the German zoo in Munich and was shot. Officials do not know how those animals escaped in the first place. The zoo has not being maintained by the municipality for over 2 years because of government budget constraints. The gates at each entry were made from iron which rusted and could be broken if enough pressure was placed. This caused the animals to go on the run while escaping through the rusted fence. Azanian Times confirms that the big cats were still within the 20 hectare grounds of the zoo when they were finally located by a drone. The Munich police department was deployed to hunt down these cats, while residents of the town were told to stay indoors.

CHAPTER 10

CHEF AKE JOLLOF THE GREAT

DEAR MKHULU,

I WENT TO GET MY DNA EXAMINED TODAY. I AM EXTREMELY INTERESTED IN FINDING OUT WHAT MY ANCESTRY ENTAILS AS IT PERTAINS TO MY HERITAGE. THE RESULTS CAME BACK AFTER 30 MINUTES STATING THAT I HAVE ANCESTRY THAT CAN BE TRACED BACK TO WEST AFRICA. MY BLOODLINE TELLS A STORY OF AN ANCESTOR FROM THE WOLOF KINGDOM OF PRESENT-DAY SENEGAL.

THIS ANCESTORS' NAME IS AKE AND WAS A VERY SKILLED CULINARY GENIUS. AKE WAS A CHEF OF EXTRAORDINARY SKILL AND TALENT IN THE KITCHEN AND COULD DO THINGS THAT ONLY A FEW AT THIS TIME COULD. IT IS ALSO SAID THAT HE IS THE AFRICAN THAT INSPIRED A MOOR IN EUROPE TO CREATE AN AUTHENTIC DINING EXPERIENCE FOR THE MOORISH ROYALS IN THE NORTH AND SOUTH.

AKE CAME FROM HUMBLE BEGINNINGS AND WAS RAISED BY A CARPENTER ALONGSIDE SEVEN SIBLINGS WITH A HOUSEWIFE FOR A MOTHER WHO LOVED AND CARED FOR THEM. HIS LOVE FOR FOOD WAS UNMATCHED AND HIS RESTAURANT IN THE CAPITAL HAD MEN AND WOMEN FROM ALL OVER THE ANCIENT WORLD ENTERING ITS DOORS FOR HIS DELICACIES.

MOYA ALSO TELLS ME OF THE YEAR THAT AKE WAS INVITED TO TAKE PART IN THE ANNUAL FEAST FOR LEGENDS COMPETITION HELD IN DAHOMEY. THIS EVENT BROUGHT THE BEST CHEFS FROM ALL OVER THE WORLD, HAILING FROM THE FOUR CORNERS OF THE SEAS.

FROM THE DYNASTIES OF CHINA, THE MOHR'S OF GERMANIA, THE DUNES OF NUBIA, THE SULTANATE OF WEST AFRICA, THE FOREST OF THE MAYA, AND THE MOUNTAINS OF THE CHEROKEE.

THE FEAST OF LEGENDS TESTED CHEFS ON THREE CATEGORIES, NAMELY: THE ENTREE ROUND, THE MAIN COURSE ROUND, AND THE DESSERT ROUND.

EACH ROUND HAD UNIQUE CHALLENGES AND OBSTACLES FOR THE CHEFS BUT AKE COMPETED THEM WITH OUTSTANDING TALENT AND DETERMINATION.

EACH CHEF WHEN ENTERING WAS SUPPOSED TO HAVE A SIGNATURE INGREDIENT THAT THEY WOULD USE THROUGHOUT THE CONTEST.

TRUTH OR MYTH

In the eastern hemisphere, Saffron Crocus (spice flower) is more expensive than gold.

AKE CHOSE RICE AND AT THAT TIME WAS NOT A POPULAR GRAIN OR DISH INGREDIENT FOR CONSUMPTION AMONGST AFRICANS OR OTHER NATIONS.

AKE STARTED MAKING DECISIONS CREATIVELY FROM HIS RECIPE BOOK FROM THE FIRST ROUND AND EVEN MANAGED TO REACH THE FINAL ROUND WHERE HE LOST AGAINST HIS FELLOW RIVAL DIM SUNG FROM ASIA. SADLY HE LOST AT THE FINAL ROUND BUT HIS SIGNATURE DISH WAS THE MOST SPOKEN ABOUT ACROSS THE CONTINENT FOR THAT SEASON.

THIS WAS SO LEGENDARY THAT HIS RIVAL DECIDED TO GO BACK TO ASIA AND MADE RICE THE STAPLE FOOD IN CHINA AND JAPAN. WHEN ASKED BY A LOCAL GRIOT WHAT THE NAME OF THE DISH WAS, HE NAMED IT JOLLOF BECAUSE IT REMINDED HIM OF THE SUNRISES OF SENEGAL.

THE "W" WAS REPLACED WITH THE "J" BECAUSE HE RESPECTED HIS NATION AND DID NOT WANT TO OUTSHINE HIS KING.

JOLLOF RICE IS ENJOYED IN WEST AFRICA TODAY AND CAN ALSO BE EATEN WITH MEAT AND MIXED VEGETABLES OF ANY KIND.

ALL THIS TALKING ABOUT FOOD IS MAKING ME HUNGRY.

SINCERELY, YOU'RE INITIATE

"There is nothing outside of yourself that can ever enable you to get better, stronger, richer, quicker, or smarter. Everything is within. Everything exists. Seek nothing outside of yourself' - Miyamoto Musashi

Dream Diary Entry

Dream Title:

____

What was the dream about?

____

____

____

____

____

Where it took place:

____

____

____

____

____

My interpretation:

____

____

____

Keywords/phrases spoken within the dream:

Dream symbols:

Note to Self:

Azanian Ti

By Richard Omar, June 20, 2008

African mother and father

A black South African couple from Hammanskraal, a rural small town in the North of Pretoria has given birth to a blonde haired, blue eyed baby with no melanin in his skin. The baby has Caucasian features and skin tone complexion. On the surface, there is nothing African about this infant. Doctors at the local clinic hypothesize that the baby is Albino though geneticists from Pretoria University has confirmed that the baby is in fact European.

Anthropologists have done studies in the past and have linked European ancestry to an African albinoid skeletal remains found in the cold hills of the Alps. They suggest that 6000 years ago an African tribe travelled from Africa to Asia and when escaping natural disasters, moved across what today is called the "silk road" into Europe. They also detail them being trapped into an ice age while moving into the northern parts of Europe from the South-east. Historians in the African intellectual community believe that this condition is not a new phenomenon.

Azanian T

By Anele Mulaudzi, July 8, 2008

Rapist murdered

A well respected police officer regarded as a fierce fighter against child abuse is found guilty by the court of murdering the man who raped his daughter. This story has sparked a division amongst South Africans after an episode of Special Investigations came out with a documentary labelled: A Fathers pride. This documentary details the killing of a man who is caught, arrested, and then shot dead by a distraught father who took retribution for the raping of his daughter. Based in Kwa-Thema, the documentary to some might have painted a picture of justice as the local police service department of the township failed to act on the raping of 16 year old Tumelo Sekhukune, so her father Mandla did what he had to do. Mandle Sekhukune was or is still to most a loving father who formed part of a neighbourhood watch programme to curb the scourge of sexual assault in the area but is now dealing with this plague first-hand.

CHAPTER 11

THE ALZHEIMER TOKOLOSHE

DEAR MKHULU,

GETTING OLD HAS ITS CHALLENGES. I CAN ALREADY SEE HOW MY GRANDPARENTS' BODIES CHANGE AS THEY HAVE BECOME ELDERLY CITIZENS. ON THE FIRST DAY OF EVERY MONTH, SENIOR CITIZENS HAVE TO TRAVEL TO EITHER THE POST OFFICE OR TO THEIR RESPECTIVE BANKS AND WAIT IN LINE TO COLLECT THEIR MONTHLY PENSION. FOR MOST ELDERLY MEMBERS OF OUR COMMUNITY, THIS MEANS THAT THEY HAVE TO SEND A LOVED ONE OR COLLECT THEIR WELFARE STIPEND ALONE BY THEMSELVES.

EARLIER THIS MONTH IN MEADOW LANDS AN INTERESTING EVENT TOOK PLACE NEAR THE SHOPPING MALL JUST TWO BLOCKS AWAY FROM THE MAIN ROAD WHERE YOU USED TO TAKE ME A COUPLE OF YEARS, BACK WHEN I WAS A KID TO PLAY ARCADE GAMES.

MOYA HAD TAKEN ME THERE TO WITNESS THE RE-ENACTMENT OF A SHADOW TOKOLOSHE. THIS TYPE OF TOKOLOSHE STEALS THE MEMORIES OF ELDERLY PEOPLE.

NO ONE UNDERSTANDS WHY IT WOULD DO SUCH A THING OR THE PURPOSE OF IT SPECIFICALLY TARGETING THIS PARTICULAR SECTION OF THE BRAIN.

WHAT I WAS SHOWN BY MOYA WAS HOW THIS AFFECTED A MAN WHO LIVED CLOSED BY. VUSI MABENA OR AS HE IS AFFECTIONATELY KNOWN BY HIS COMMUNITY "NTATE MABENA". VUSI GREW UP TO BECOME A RESPECTED LEADER OF HIS NEIGHBOURHOOD. HE LOVED JAZZ MUSIC AND HAD A BEAUTIFUL BIG FAMILY.

EVEN THOUGH THEY HAD LESS, THEY WERE HAPPY AND CONTENT.

VUSI MABENA HAD ALWAYS LOVED LIVING IN THE NOISY STREETS OF SOWETO WITH ITS SLOBBERING, OVER-LAPPING SHACKS SCATTERED ACROSS THE TOWNSHIP HORIZON. IT WAS A PLACE WHERE HE FELT CALM.

HE DIGRESSED FROM NEGATIVITY BY REMAINING SPIRITUALLY FAITHFUL TO HIS TRADITIONAL CULTURAL PRACTICES. HE WAS AN ARROGANT, SMART, BRANDY DRINKER WITH SLIMY ARMS.

HIS FRIENDS SAW HIM AS A TALENTED TEACHER.

BEING AN EXORCIST, HIM AND HIS CHURCH WOULD HELP OLD PEOPLE LIKE THEMSELVES UNDERGO CLEANSING RITUALS IN THEIR HOMES TO END THE CYCLES OF GENERATIONAL CURSES AS TO END THE KARMIC HARM THAT COULD AFFECT THEIR LOVED ONES OR OFFSPRING.

MOYA SHOWED ME NTATE VUSI HAD MET A MIDDLE-AGED WOMAN ONE DAY WHO WAS SEEKING HIS HELP ON HEALING HER MOTHER

FROM AN UNKNOWN CONDITION THAT COULD NOT BE DIAGNOSED BY WESTERN DOCTORS. NTATE VUSI DECIDED TO ASSIST AND WENT TO THIS WOMAN'S HOME WITH A ZULU TRANSLATED BIBLE AND TWO WHITE CANDLES.

ONCE HE GOT INTO THE BEDROOM WHERE THE OLD MOTHER WAS LYING QUIETLY, VUSI WALKED OVER TO THE WINDOW AND REFLECTED ON HIS DIRTY SURROUNDINGS.

THE OLD LADY WAS TOO PARALYZED TO MOVE ON THE BED BUT THE BEDROOM LOOKED LIKE A TORNADO HAD VISITED THE HOUSE BEFORE HE ARRIVED THERE. MOYA EXPLAINED THAT THIS MESS WAS CREATED BY THE MEMORY STEALING TOKOLOSHE AND HAS BEEN SLEEPING UNDER THE BED FOR THE PAST THREE YEARS.

MOYA ALSO PSYCHICALLY SHOWED ME THE TOKOLOSHE EMERGING OUT OF A HUMAN SHADOW FROM THE WINDOW OF THE BEDROOM AND WITH ITS LONG FINGERS STROKING THE OLD LADY'S HAIR AT NIGHT. NTATE VUSI NOTICED TOO. HE OPENED A SCRIPTURE AND READ A VERSE BACKWARD QUICKLY BEFORE THE TOKOLOSHE COULD HIDE WITHIN ITS SHADOW. THE GROUND SHOOK WHILE THE HAIL POUNDED LIKE A SHOWER OF BULLETS OUTSIDE THE HOUSE.

AT THIS SUPERNATURAL MOMENT, NTATE VUSI ENCOUNTERED AN ANCESTRAL SPIRIT LONG FORGOTTEN BY THE FAMILY OF THIS WOMAN AND HER ELDERLY MOTHER. A BRIGHT LIGHT EXPLODED THROUGH

THE WINDOWS AND CURTAINS OF THE BEDROOM AND BLASTED INTO THE BEDROOM. THEN HE SAW SOMETHING IN THE DISTANCE, OR RATHER SOMEONE.

IT WAS THE FIGURE OF DINEO, THE LOST THIRD-BORN DAUGHTER OF THE WOMAN.

THIS WAS NOT HER IN THE FLESH BUT A HOLOGRAPHIC IMAGE OF HER WALKING TOWARDS HIM IN SPIRITUAL FORM.

DINEO STOOD NEXT TO VUSI AND TOLD HIM WHICH SPIRITUAL POINT OF CONTACT TO USE IN THE VANQUISHING OF THE TOKOLOSHE. VUSI GULPED AS HE WAS NOT PREPARED AT SEEING A GHOST SO CLEARLY BEFORE.

BOTH THE WOMAN AND HER MOTHER COULD NOT SEE WHAT WAS HAPPENING BECAUSE IT HAPPENED AT A BRIEF INSTANT.

TRUTH OR MYTH

In Southern African mythology, a tokoloshe is a trickster demon that can be vanquished with sea salt.

MOYA TELLS ME THAT DINEO WAS A SPIRITUALLY INTUITIVE INDIVIDUAL WITH A WITTY PERSONALITY BUT WAS KIDNAPPED AND RAPED WHEN SHE WAS YOUNG. NONETHELESS HER DEATH DID NOT MEAN HER SPIRIT STOPPED MATURING.

DINEO CONTINUED TO GROW IN THE ANCESTRAL PLAIN AND MANIFESTED HERSELF WITHIN THE ZULU BIBLE WHERE SHE WAS WAITING TO BE UNLEASHED SO SHE COULD HELP HER FAMILY AGAINST SPIRITUAL ATTACKS.

VUSI WAS THEN TOLD TO CLOSE HIS EYES SO SHE COULD PRAY FOR HIM AND ANOINT HIM WITH THE POWER OF VANQUISHING THE TOKOLOSHE. WHEN HE OPENED HIS EYES EVERYTHING WAS BACK TO NORMAL.

VUSI BEGAN THE RITUAL AND AFTER 12 MINUTES WAS DONE. THE OLD LADY FELL ASLEEP AND LUNCH WAS THEN PREPARED FOR EVERYONE.

AS VUSI STEPPED OUTSIDE DINEO REAPPEARED TO HIM AND CAME CLOSER, HE COULD SEE A SHADOW SLOWLY FADING INTO THE AFTERNOON PAVEMENT OF SOWETO.

DINEO TOLD VUSI ABOUT THE TOKOLOSHE AND SAID IT WAS NOT DESTROYED AS YOU CANNOT DESTROY ENERGY BUT ONLY CONTAIN IT. THE TOKOLOSHE WENT BACK TO THE POST OFFICE OUTSIDE THE

SHOPPING MALL AREA AND HAS BEEN TAKING MEMORIES FROM THE INNOCENT SENIOR CITIZENS EVER SINCE.

THIS PESTERING DEMON HAS NOT BEEN CONTAINED YET. MOYA HAS NOW INVOLVED US IN THIS MISSION TO CONTAIN THIS SPIRIT INSIDE A SPIRIT BOTTLE.

I WILL GO AND PURCHASE A BOTTLE OF BRANDY TOMORROW MORNING AND CALL UPON THE OLD ONES TO HELP US BEFORE WE BEGIN.

AS I WRITE YOU THIS LETTER, I CAN ALREADY SENSE THE TOKOLOSHE GAINING ITS STRENGTH.

SEE YOU SOON,

SINCERELY, YOU'RE INITIATE

"A beautiful woman should break her mirror early" - Balthasar Gracian

Dream Diary Entry

Dream Title:

What was the dream about?

Where it took place:

My interpretation:

Keywords/phrases spoken within the dream:

Dream symbols:

Note to Self:

Azanian T

By Justin Baker, July 14, 2008

Instagram models fuel plas

Many young girls today are flocking towards cosmetic surgery and opting for a Brazilian butt lift which was the hottest growing plastic surgery procedure last year. In South Africa more than 18 million people had some sort of cosmetic procedure done last year, including Botox injections in the facial area. Many aspire to look good on Instagram, millennials inspired by African female curves helped drive a record number of Brazilian butt lifts and a booming plastic surgery market in Mzansi.

Butt augmentation also seemed to be popular last year. This procedure lets women take unwanted fat from one area like the stomach and add it to the back side. A whopping surge of 19 percent with 24,000 procedures done in 2007. The previous record was only 19,000 a year earlier. Millennials primarily in East Europe and other developing Anglo nations in particular tell doctors they want to look as good in person as they do through their Snapchat filters and on image editing apps.

Azanian Ti

By Rumi Ahmed, August 4, 2008

White women threatened b

Many women of African descent age slower than their European counter parts. Studies from the Sankofa Institute of Melanin have proven that a 50 year old African woman will look much younger than a 40 year old white woman. As most of their faces start showing the visible signs of aging, many black woman's faces seems to remain the same. The Sankofa institute has also said that black woman age slower but will eventually look older as time progresses. One of the surveys conducted by the institute details the life of Carol Johnson an attractive African American woman who claims white women have always felt a sense of envy towards black women, and as she ages, it seems to be getting much worse. From the random comments about why can't she just age like the rest of them, to the aggressive glance, I've been through it all. Carol has stated in one of her vlogs that white women are desired by white men and black men and she does not understand why white women are jealous of her.

CHAPTER 12

DO VAMPIRES EXIST? : A MEMOIR

DEAR MKHULU,

WE BOTH KNOW THAT CULTS HAVE ALWAYS EXISTED AROUND THE WORLD. THESE OCCURRENCES OF THESE GROUPS OF PEOPLE HAVE SOMEHOW SPORADICALLY SPREAD SINCE THE DAWN OF THE MILLENNIUM. CULTS IN AFRICA HAVE ONLY BEEN RELEGATED IN SMALL POCKETS WITHIN INDIGENOUS COMMUNITIES IN THE PAST BUT SINCE THE INDUSTRIAL ERA, WE BEGAN TO SEE THEM MAKE THEIR WAY SECRETLY AMONGST INDUSTRIES, PLACES OF WORSHIP, AND EVEN IN HIGHER ACADEMIC INSTITUTIONS.

IN WESTERN MYTHOLOGY, WE ARE INTRODUCED TO THE CONCEPT OF THE VAMPIRE, WHICH IS A NOCTURNAL CREATURE WHO WAS BITTEN ON THE NECK BY ANOTHER AND HAD THEIR BLOOD SUCKED FROM THEIR VEINS.

THIS CONTROVERSIALLY CAN ALSO BE BASED ON THE MEDIEVAL STORY OF "VLAD THE IMPALER" AN ARMY GENERAL IN EUROPEAN HISTORY WHO DESPISED THE TURKS SO MUCH THAT WHEN HE KILLED THEM IN WAR, HE WOULD IMPALE THEIR BODIES ON A WOODEN STAKE AND DRINK THE BLOOD DRIPPING FROM THEM BELIEVING THAT CONSUMING THE BLOOD OF HIS ENEMY MADE HIM POWERFUL.

THIS TO ME AT FIRST WAS BIZARRE BUT GROWING UP I HAVE ALWAYS HAD A FEELING THAT VAMPIRES ARE REAL. I REMEMBER SEEING STRANGE THINGS DURING MY UNIVERSITY YEARS. I REMEMBER A GROUP OF STUDENTS WHO I ENCOUNTERED WHILE AT THE COMMUNE INSIDE THE CAMPUS ON WHICH I WAS LIVING.

THE LEADER OF THIS GROUP WAS THOMAS SITHOLE A RESPECTED MEMBER OF THE SRC (STUDENT REPRESENTATIVE COUNCIL) AND TALENTED UNIVERSITY CHOIR VOCALIST. THOMAS AND HIS FRIENDS GOT ALONG WITH EVERYBODY AND SEEMED TO BE YOUNG GIFTED AND BLACK STUDENTS WITH THEIR WHOLE LIVES AHEAD OF THEM.

SINCE MOST YOUNG PEOPLE AT THAT AGE VALUE FAME, MOST OF THE STUDENTS THAT LIVED OUTSIDE OF CAMPUS HAVE ALWAYS WORSHIPED THEM. YOU COULD SEE HOW THEY WERE ALWAYS HANGING OUT AT THE STUDENT CENTRE NEXT TO THE MAIN COMMUNE WHERE WE USED TO STAY.

I BEING IN THAT COMMUNE WAS PURELY BY COINCIDENCE AS I GOT PLACED THERE BY A CAMPUS COORDINATOR WHO FILLED MY ACCOMMODATION INFORMATION IN THE WRONG FOLDERS AND CAUSED A MIX-UP WITH MY SETTLEMENT DOCUMENTATION.

SO, I DECIDED TO RATHER STAY SINCE IT WAS ALSO CLOSE TO MY LECTURE HALLS AND MY FAVOURITE BURGER OUTLET.

IN THE FIRST FEW MONTHS, I WAS GETTING SETTLED IN VARSITY LIFE AND NEVER WITNESSED WHAT WAS TAKING PLACE AROUND ME. I WAS ALSO NOT YET ON MY PATH OF INITIATION SO MY ABILITIES TO COMMUNICATE WITH MOYA WERE NOT STRONG AT THAT TIME. ONCE I HUNG OUT AT THE COMMUNE MORE, I STARTED NOTICING STRANGE BEHAVIOUR. THOMAS'S CREW WERE NEVER IN THEIR DORM ROOMS DURING THE NIGHT BUT WERE ALWAYS ASLEEP IN THE AFTERNOON.

WHEN ASKED ABOUT THIS ONE NIGHT HE MADE A JOKE AND SAID THEY LIVE LIKE BATS. DURING THE WINTER THEY WOKE UP AT NIGHT AND I COULD HEAR PEOPLE WHISPERING THROUGH THE HALLS.

THEY ONLY WENT OUTSIDE IN THE AFTERNOON WHEN THEY WENT TO CLASS AND WHEN THEY CHILLED AT THE STUDENT CENTRE, BUT ALWAYS IN THE SHADE. I THOUGHT IT WAS THE HEAT BUT THEY CONTINUED THIS BEHAVIOUR EVEN UNTIL THE WINTER WHICH WAS INTERESTING FOR ME.

I IGNORED THESE SIGNS AND CARRIED ON WITH MY LIFE BUT WEEKS AFTER MY MIDTERM TEST CYCLE, PECULIAR EVENTS STARTED TAKING PLACE AMONGST THEM.

FOR SOME REASON, MOYA KEPT WARNING ME TO STAY AWAY FROM THEM THROUGH DREAMS AND SIMILARLY WARNED ME NOT TO LEAVE MY FOOD IN THE KITCHEN BECAUSE THEY COULD TAMPER WITH IT.

DAYS AFTER MY DREAM, I STARTED NOTICING PEOPLE WHO WOULD BEFRIEND THEM DISAPPEAR FROM CAMPUS LITTLE BY LITTLE.

THIS WAS WEIRD AS NO INVESTIGATION OF THESE STUDENTS WAS CONDUCTED ON CAMPUS.

THEY WERE LAST SEEN WITH THESE VICTIMS BUT NONE OF THEM APPEARED IN COURT.

ON ONE AFTERNOON WHILE I WAS STUDYING FOR THE WINTER EXAMS IN THE LIBRARY A BEAUTIFUL TALL YOUNG LADY CAME UP TO ME AND SAID SHE HAD SOMETHING VERY INTERESTING TO TELL ME.

BEING ATTRACTED TO HER, WE WALKED OUTSIDE AND SAT BY THE FOUNTAIN.

TRUTH OR MYTH

Certain empaths can feel if someone is an energy extractor or not.

SHE BURST INTO TEARS AND BEGAN TO EXPRESS HOW TERRIFIED SHE WAS FOR HER SAFETY SINCE SHE BELIEVED VAMPIRES WERE OUT TO GET HER.

THIS PRETTY LADY THEN SPOKE ABOUT SOME SRC MEMBERS IN VARSITY BEING PART OF A CULT WHEREBY THEY JOIN THIS CULT IN PURSUIT OF POPULARITY AND SOCIAL DOMINANCE.

THIS ALL MADE SENSE TO ME.

SHE FURTHERMORE STATED THAT CERTAIN SECTIONS OF THE CAMPUS BELONGED TO THIS CULT OF VAMPIRES AND THEY MEET DURING THE NIGHT AS THEY SLEEP IN THE EARLY AFTERNOON. IT TURNS OUT THESE VAMPIRES ARE DIFFERENT FROM THE ONES WE READ ABOUT FOR THEY HAVE MELANIN, SO THEY ARE SOMEWHAT PROTECTED FROM THE SUN DEPENDING ON HOW LONG THEY HAVE BEEN VAMPIRES.

AFTER SPEAKING WITH THIS LADY, I ASKED AROUND THE CAMPUS AND WENT BACK HOME TO MEDITATE SO THAT I COULD RECEIVE DIRECTION FROM MOYA.

3 HOURS LATER, A BLUE CRANE BIRD ENTERED MY WINDOW WITH A SMALL NOTE IN ITS BEAK. IT SPAT IT OUT AND FLEW OUT THE ROOM.

THE NOTE READ:

"THE NAME OF THE CULT IS CALLED THE COVENANT AND THEY ARE COMPRISED OF A GROUP OF YOUNG PEOPLE WHO ARE MADE VAMPIRES BY DRINKING A CONCOCTION THEY RECEIVE FROM AN ASIAN WET MARKET SOMEWHERE IN GAUTENG. THESE PEOPLE RECRUIT MEMBERS BY KIDNAPPING THEM AND INUNDATING THEM WITH A DRUG.

THEY ARE HIRED BY POWERFUL POLITICIANS AND DO THEIR BIDDING IN EXCHANGE FOR CORPORATE ACCESS TO UPPER ECHELON JOBS AND EXTRAVAGANT MATERIAL POSSESSIONS.

SOME OF THEM ARE ALSO RECRUITED TO PROVIDE POWERFUL PEOPLE WITH SINISTER FETISHES LIKE PEDOPHILIA AND REVENGE ASSASSINATIONS. THIS BLOOD MAKES THEM STRONG AND THEIR NUMBERS ARE EXPANDING AMONGST YOUNG PEOPLE.

THE ONES YOU ARE AMONGST ARE DOING THESE THINGS BECAUSE THEY ARE BEING PROMISED ENTRANCE INTO THE POLITICAL ELITE CIRCLES"

I WAS FURTHER WARNED AT THE BACK OF THE NOTE TO NOT SPEAK OF THIS TO ANYONE AND TO NOT INTERFERE IN THIS EVER AGAIN AS I WAS NOT POWERFUL ENOUGH AT THAT TIME TO CONDUCT SPIRITUAL WARS.

MOYA ENCOURAGES ME TO TAKE ON THIS CULT IF I INTEND TO GO

BACK TO VARSITY TO COMPLETE MY MASTER'S DEGREE ONCE THE FINAL STAGES OF MY INITIATION ARE DONE.

NOT MUCH CAN BE SAID ABOUT THIS, ONLY THAT WE HAVE TO BE CAREFUL MOVING FORWARD.

THE SHADOW IS WINNING.

WE NEED TO BE VIGILANT.

SINCERELY, YOU'RE INITIATE

"Your children are not your children. They are the sons and daughters of life's longing for itself. They come through you but not from you, and though they are with you yet they belong not to you" - Kahlil Gibran

Dream Diary Entry

Dream Title:

____

What was the dream about?

____

____

____

____

____

Where it took place:

____

____

____

____

____

My interpretation:

____

____

____

Keywords/phrases spoken within the dream:

Dream symbols:

Note to Self:

Acknowledgements

I would like to take this moment to acknowledge my paternal and maternal ancestry.

The Lekhethoa and Mathapo family who I descend from.

Without these four fathers and four mothers, I would not be able to properly articulate my artistic abilities.

I appreciate those that came before me as they are my gift from the creator. It is the blood that flows in me that I can continue.

Praise be to you.

About the Author

Three words best describe Thabang H.A Mathapo...

STORYTELLING, ART, and SPIRITUALITY...

Thabang H. A Mathapo is an author with a good eye for aesthetic artistry and literary excellence.

A native from the City of Tshwane – a prolific city situated in the Gauteng province of South Africa, he can't help but let his upbringing spill on a page. In 2015 he was awarded a National Diploma in Public Relations and communications management from the University of Johannesburg and began his academic journey.

He is a loyal patron of media and literature with an O.C.D addiction to mythology.

He is a thinker and prides himself in being a sigma male with him spending days with a pen and paper writing stories that will transcend time and space.

He is not a hero nor a villain but an intellectual rebel who will surely create outstanding contributions to the global human family.

Thabang is a 2020 – 2021 Debut programme graduate of Business Arts South Africa.

<u>**Author Contact info**</u>

Current contacts:

Email = nativebookz@gmail.com

Twitter = @ThabangArt1

Instagram = thabangart

Facebook = Thabang Amun

WhatsApp Business = +27 67 867 2157

This book has been supported by Business Arts South Africa in partnership with the South African department of sports, arts and culture.

www.ingramcontent.com/pod-product-compliance
Lightning Source LLC
La Vergne TN
LVHW010616100826
845148LV00014B/2987

* 9 7 8 0 6 2 0 9 2 8 7 9 3 *